The Forgotten Chronicles of Edward Davenport

The Tenth Muse of Mytilene

"You may forget but let me tell you this; someone in some future time will think of us."

-Sappho

The Davenport Chronicle of Archaeology was founded in 1901 by aspiring historian Edward Davenport and the generous supporter of nearly a hundred expeditions, Archibald Wescott. For decades, Davenport and Wescott maintained the journal and produced thirty-two research articles detailing their impossible discoveries from around the world, reforming the field of archaeology.

The Chronicle was closed for publication in 1924 after the untimely death of Wescott and the collapse of his estate.

This issue recites Edward's first published expedition that has since been forgotten by our world…

Chapter 01

Although I find Richard Gunther to be a good man and an excellent cricket player, the truth of the matter is this. He has no right excavating the Temple of Serapis. In his recent article, published in this very journal, his actual first observation made upon the temple's grounds was that the structures were perfectly preserved due to the tide's encroachment on the temple. Now, Gunther's observations should have first and foremost been made during his time at Winchester while sitting by his fireplace drinking some bourbon and reading local Italian reports straight from Pozzuoli. However, men like Gunther lack the patience and the etiquette to labor over texts that are not their own. So, I will address the main error which lies in Gunther's logic.

Yes, the sediment brought in by the tide would help preserve the base of the largest Serapeum in the ancient world, yet the damage had already been done by the corrosive salt water. Months of labor, likely from Greco-

Egyptian slaves, would have possibly been diminished by Poseidon's willful waters! And now, due to the laziness of one archaeologist who refused to dam up the advancement of the sea, who knows how much more will be lost before the next expedition!

Gunther offers new, bright-eyed potential to the study of archaeology, yet his first concern should always be focused on the preservation of the site as well as its environment. To blindly walk to the shores of Italy with the intention of sketching some drawings and kicking about sand is like sailing a ship from port with no destination in mind.

This was the Temple of Serapis! The precursor to the Library of Alexandria, which is still a complete and total mystery to our study! All procedures must be taken before, during, and after an excavation to protect what our ancestors have left behind. To the hobbyists, I beg you reconsider this field. To my colleagues, I encourage you to think and plan before you step foot on an ancient site. And to Gunther, perhaps you should re-read my article on the

moral obligation and ethics of archaeologists before

adventuring out again.

Edward Davenport

After signing my name on the end of my research, I laid

back in my red upholstered chair that I had picked up in

Austria on a fishing trip. The smells of sour coffee floated

throughout the study, dust collecting on the top shelves of

filled-out bookcases. What had started as a warm Autumn

night had shined the once velvet blanket into the dawning

orange sky. Sleep pulled at the back of my tired ocular

nerves, but I continued to busy myself with carefully

reading over my writing once more. I had stayed up late

finishing an article in response to Gunther's excavation

report that had come out in the *Archaeologia* at the opening

of 1901. My intentions were not to attack or discourage the

youth's hopeful ambition as Gunther had frequently asked for my opinion on his findings in Pozzuoli, but it is hard to disregard his naivety towards site management. The boy's promise was soiled by a cluttered mind.

My eyes rested on the last sentence with a feeling of dissatisfaction. Rushed. Untidy. If I had one more week, another day even, then I know that I could produce a more substantial and educative argument for the journal. Yet, I didn't have any more time for embellishment. The *Archaeologia* antiquarian journal had requested new material from me as I had not sent anything for publishing in the last nine months. Partly because I had refused every excavation opportunity offered to me. I had seen enough grave desecration from my time at Oxford University. The thought of contributing to the same flawed practices I denounced felt repulsive. However, that was not the only reason I had rejected every prospect handed my way.

At first, I thought I was ill and in need of rest. Yet, my idleness hadn't cleared up overnight. Consequently, I figured it to be a brief stint. Yet, these past nine months I have lacked all ambition for my studies. Each journal I've read, each excavation I heard of; none of it felt like there was any impact on our world. No one cared about the discovery of Knossos and its throne room which was already bearing more information on our understanding of ancient languages than anything in the history of archaeology. No one cared about the Temple of Eshmun which was violated by the Roman Empire, or the Catacombs of Kom El Shoqafa in Egypt, or even the Antikythera shipwreck with one of the oddest devices crafted by human hands. No one truly cared about the effort behind reconstructing the ancient world and uncovering her mysteries.

There was no concern for our own history.

With a furrowed brow, I neatly placed my research paper into an envelope, wrapping the twine taut so as to not let the papers fly out. Then, a chime from out in the corridor reverberated through my eardrums. I raced over to a parting gift from my father, a tall Greenwich wall clock whose face was wide and flat. The hour hand had just struck six, bellowing six sing-song chimes.

Cambridge had opened its gates only an hour ago now, which would give Eloise and Oscar Pemberley of the *Archaeologia* a chance to have their morning tea and cakes before setting up articles for the newest issue. There wasn't much time now until the winter edition would be sent out over the holidays, and I would miss out on another chance at publication. Not like they would give me such a chance since the husband-and-wife duo were notoriously difficult with my own writing after the last time I brought them a few dozen photos. They had refused to print more than two images of my work since the printing cost wasn't worth, and I quote, 'piles of human feces that held no interest to readers.'

I was researching the waste piles of Neolithic man in the caves of Northern France, but to be fair; those pictures were necessary for my thesis on early man's dietary health.

This time, I had elected to keep a single photograph in my envelope. One that I had borrowed from my colleague, Archie Wescott, which depicted Gunther hilariously rummaging through mud with his bare hands to clear off the Ptolemaic pillars.

The sixth and final chime rang out, bringing me back to my corridor, and reminding me how terribly late I was.

As I was rushing around my small estate, picking up my overcoat and top hat from my closet, I glided down the stairs with envelope in hand and nearly was out the door without my treasured ebony walking stick. Another gift from my father, the walking stick held a Victorian brass handle with a sterling silver inlay in the shape of a flying Goldfinch.

It was a short stride into town, yet enough time had passed for my mind to wander with my gait through the English countryside. I thought back to last Spring, which was dreadfully stormier than I had hoped. The rain had made it nearly impossible to explore the moors with the Romanian excavation team that we had planned for months. Instead, I stayed inside reading awful articles from archaeologists just out of university trying to make a point. Most of what they published was rubbish. Claims with no context. Quite absurd theories. Yet, their methods, although differing, were extraordinary to study. The way in which students approached different sites in order to gather their own evidence.

Perhaps that could make a good article for—

"Eight! No, let's say seven."

Startled, I took a step back. "Seven pounds," shouted between browned teeth, a sweaty gale.

Lost in thought, I failed to recognize that I had arrived at the stagecoach in town. A stout coach driver had stepped down from his stoop and was feeding his horses from a pail while looking me up and down. Straightening my stance, I reached into my coat to grab my coin purse. "I need a ride to Cambridge. Quickly, if you can."

He smiled between chapped lips. "These are the fastest Hackneys you'll find; they are!"

I parted with some change and helped myself into this man's stagecoach. Moments after some shuffling in the front, a howl and the stamping of hooves sent the wagon forward.

It was just under five hours spent in that death-trap of a cabin before the rolling green offered in the wagon door's window parted way for short buildings lining up half-cobblestoned streets. They were done in the same manner as the new structures sprouting up in London, a revival of Gothic arches and parapets. It was all a lot of attractive stonework. Maybe in a few years it would be as big as London, but now it still held some of the old world. An antique wooden bridge crossed over the slow river that crossed through town. Its beams were angular, something more French than British. A few people were currently crossing, paying no mind to the architecture under their feet. They simply chatted and walked across.

The stagecoach dropped me off near King's College in the center of the university and I paid the man an extra pound to wait whilst I conducted my business. He wasn't too thrilled at the prospect of sitting and feeding his horses while potential customers passed him by, but he agreed when he saw the coin in my palm.

Cambridge University was like a perfectly planned maze. The multiple colleges constructed for the University spanned the course of five centuries and around three dozen architects, each with their own style in structure. The squares were beautiful, if only a bit symmetrical. Cascading brushes and vines climbed the stone walls with colorful flowers on their backs. Statues in honor of past alumni lined the walkways, each with a plaque reminding the students why they were important enough to earn a statue. Only those the college were proud of calling their own received that luxury.

There were no anthropologists on display.

I neared one of the libraries which also housed the classic's department for the university. I had spent many hours roaming its halls as a student, carefully reading through original ancient texts and speaking the old tongues fluently. The mere thought of seeing those early writings again probably struck fear into my colleagues. However, it instead ignited some of that lost ambition. To breathe in the crusty air of the library, feel the leather pages still covered in soil; I felt like a student once more.

The beautiful language of Homer and Ovid and Plato! A sense of sound mind in a world of myth! To travel with Odysseus and his crew across the Mediterranean Sea, to watch the Greek deities launch into battle with the titans! In these texts, I felt more at ease than I did in my own living room.

"Mr. Davenport?" a woman's voice croaked past busied students.

I turned to find Eloise Pemberley in her professor's frock and cap with a stack of papers in her hands. She was slightly younger than myself, a blonde, grew up with a kind family sitting nicely with a wealthy estate, and she also refused help from me on her dissertation since I was often too critical of her work. I'm still not sure if I was insulted or amused when she declined my offer.

"Eloise," I smiled. "Where is Oscar? I've written up a new report which I think he'll find more than interesting."

She did not smile. Her hand waved me over to the back of the library and we ascended to the next floor where professors spent hours reading over the same essays every year. Oscar Pemberley was doing just that.

A similar stack of papers sat in the middle of his oak desk, him sitting in a green upholstered chair with some spectacles across the bridge of his nose. Oscar was much older than me, the first signs of age in the gray of his hair. He was never one to go out into the field and study antiquity sites but loved to judge how others managed their own fieldwork from his cozy chair. He had married Eloise in May of last year and I was surprised to receive an invitation. It was a nice wedding. A lovely floral display, but few from their families made appearances which was a bit peculiar at the time.

I stuck out my hand. "Oscar, how goes it?"

He shook my hand in turn. "I'm afraid many of my pupils refuse to listen. They've all completely disregarded the law of superposition, something I believe any intelligent life is aware of."

I took a chair across from him and Eloise stood beside her husband. "Yes, well, I can see how a few might find it difficult to understand that a bottle cap is younger than a Roman breastplate."

That got a smile out of him. "Perhaps I should make another class out of it. Task them with bringing me the oldest thing they can find and have them arrange the artifacts in class."

"Now, there's a thought!"

Eloise presented the new stack of papers to Oscar and excused herself from the room, shutting the door behind her. The friendly air grew stale by the second.

"Edward, I sure hope you have something good for me. The journal… well, we really need to see some improvement from your finds."

I nodded. "Of course, Oscar. I decided on writing in response to Gunther's recent excavation at the Temple of Serapis. I think you'll find his naivety and failure to preserve the dig site a sure sign to reform the standards of procedure for the entire field."

"We'll see about that."

He stared at my papers for ten minutes. Unblinking. A tapping of his booted foot on the hard wood floors. I eyed up his collection of arrowheads from the Americas. Each shape remarkably different from the last. Whether it be an angular base and narrow point or rounded base and wide point, they each carried an air of otherworldliness.

So, why were they here? Why were they locked away up here in Pemberley's office? Was he stealing their historical value for himself? Or maybe they just weren't getting the appreciation they deserved at the museum?

Perhaps Pemberley might be the only one who did care for them and that was why they were hanging up in his room in Cambridge instead of remaining buried back in the Americas. Still, who was Pemberley to decide whether an artifact was important to our studies or not?

Whatever the case, they certainly didn't belong in an English university.

A heavy sigh flowed free from Pemberley's lips. "Edward…"

The tone of his voice was enough for me to get the gist of his reading. "What? What was wrong with my argument this time?"

"Edward, the magazine doesn't tend to post responses. The point is for you to go out yourself, find something out about the ancient world, and report it back to the public. Not denounce your colleagues. And especially not the paper or the college who fund your research.”

“Sir, Gunther is a good friend. I have helped him out on multiple occasions. I did not intend to reprimand his actions, merely point out how we, as a study, need to improve our methods. Research needs to be done off site first and foremost! I feel this is a rule that will help save countless personal records and artifacts from being trampled on by half-cocked grave robbers!”

“The point!” Pemberley raised his voice. “The point of this paper is to actually *do* research. You have only criticized and denounced the actions of your colleagues for an entire year!”

“No, I am trying to improve our standards—”

Pemberley slammed his hand down onto the desk, shaking the tower of papers apart from their organized stack. “Don’t try and cover up your inactivity with excuses! It's pitiable, Edward."

His words held back bile in his voice box, articulating it with a short cough. I was a tad stunned by the professor's volatility. Never before had he spoken to me with such 'tough-love' talk in my past attempts at publication. I fell further and further into the comfort of my chair.

Oscar shook his head, regaining his composure. "I'm troubled by your lack of initiative, Edward. The entire board is too. They want to revoke your funding."

"What?" I gasped. "You can't let them do this, Oscar. I-I— I have done so much for the journal and the university in years past. I've… I've, well, just hit a small wall. Let me write something new."

He sighed. He sighed with finality. "I can't keep giving you chances, Edward."

I leaned forward in my chair to lock eyes with Oscar, his own were a golden brown trapped in the body of schoolteacher. I just about pleaded, begged, and intreated him for one last chance.

"One last chance. Just give me that, Pemberley…"

He was as still as the Greek marbles locked away only one floor beneath our feet. An impenetrable look of judgement and thought. Then, a gracious nod. "One chance. I can only give you one month, before the winter magazine needs to be finalized and sent off to the presses."

I rounded the table and brought the man into a hug. He seemed unconvinced by my sincereness, but I still thanked him countless times on my way out the door.

One chance. One month to discover an artifact that will impress the unenthusiastic *Archaeologia*.

One month to fall back in love with my despised.

Fieldwork.

Chapter 02

It had been close to three days after my trip to Cambridge when I realized that there was absolutely no possible way that I would uncover an ancient mystery locked in the confines of my own estate. No more critiques of my colleagues' destructive methods would satisfy the hypercritical gaze of a magazine editor. Instead, I would have to venture out of my comfortable setting in search of something more primordial.

At least, that is what I believed when I set out of my home and entered the colorful greenery of Somerset. The fading summer still kept the evening air warm and windy, yet the grasses and trees started to show the first shedding of leaves and adorned a yellowing hue. The once brazen green hills where early man once settled, were now dominated by abhorrent last century summer homes. Buildings brimming with life now would no doubt cease to flourish in a week or two when the cold came, and the structures fell into winter ruins. There were few like me who stayed in Somerset all year round. Besides my colleague and friend, Archie Wescott, there were only the Wilhelm's, a German brood who made their money in trade across the channel. They were often kind enough to let me walk their grounds so long as I showed them what I found. Most times it was rubbish that they let me keep willingly. However, once I found an engraved silver locket in a field of southern marsh orchids and, after I relinquished what was found on their property, the family rushed off to town to figure its value.

I doubt they still have that locket. It was most likely in the hands of some private collector by now.

The sun was high in the sky at this hour, and I took the beautiful day as an opportunity to explore the woods between mine and the Wilhelm's estate. Kilometers of British timber were hardly found near the coasts of England after the hundreds of years our nation spent in shipbuilding. The forest was a worthy find in itself, but its survival wasn't its only merit. An untouched forest meant lesser chances for treasure hunters to comb this part of England.

"Meaning more chances for me to find something for the journal," I spoke aloud without realizing.

My train of thought halted for a second at the sound of my own voice.

Sometimes when I find myself lost on a tangent, the words form better on the tongue. Thankfully, I was alone. It has happened to me on a few occasions where I was entertaining company and they've gone on to calling me a *nutter* or the likes behind my back.

I stopped by a small break in the woods, feeling the fresh air fill my lungs before releasing a deep, cleansing breath back out into the wild. My eyes scanned each direction and I smiled more than I had in months. I had become absolutely lost with no idea which direction was back home.

This was the adventure I needed. The feeling of being out of my depth, cut off from my books and research. Just a natural site all to myself.

I started analyzing the earth beneath my feet, poking and prodding gently with the toe of my boot to turn over any bit of turf looking ready to come loose. Then, I made a mental map of the area by measuring out approximately fifteen meters in either direction. Taking each of my shoes, I plopped one down on either end of this row so as to not overstep my makeshift grid. After my perimeter was established, I simply started to observe.

No more kicking or prodding. No digging. I just hunched over a square yard at a time and stared down at the ground. I watched how the earth bent upward into a small hillock or how a tree's roots bulged free from the dirt to see what the fuss was about above the surface. Grass clumped up like weeds in a flower bed. Dirt softened in divots and dried up around pebbles and rounded stones. The sunlight dimmed and the shade under the forest's canopy stretched farther across my own dig site.

That's when, under the shade near my sixth grid, I found an artifact. I dared not move it right away, but I could just tell from the chipping of the flint rock present in a bed of river stones that I had found some tool. Whether it was an arrowhead or a spearhead, it was impossible to tell since most of its body was still lodged in the Earth.

Should I remove it?

Whether I did or not, someone surely would find it sooner or later. Better someone like myself than some thief looking to sell it.

I stopped, looking further around my surroundings. I looked past my charted barrier and saw a short hill with no trees on its surface. Various rocks made a loose-fitting wall around the hill and the image of the past faded into my world. A structure was beneath that mound of dirt.

Something old. Likely a campsite or perhaps storage for firewood and logs. Either way, this area had been inhabited. Maybe there were more artifacts nearby. Maybe even a whole settlement!

I started to get so excited that I nearly lost all reason. So, I took a breath to slow myself down. There were woods throughout this area. Few clearings, which made it unlikely any inhabitants lived near here. This hill was likely just a hill, and those rocks were all rounded due to the old riverbed that ran through here. There was no site here. No make-believe settlement. Now was not a time for dreaming, Edward.

I bent down and ripped the tool up from the dirt. It was chipped at the end, likely knapped with one of those river rocks. A tool made on the move to another location and thrown in the river when it broke.

That or it was just another rock.

Doubt stretched a shadow over the stone in my hand. Without further digging and research, there was no telling.

I dropped it and found a seat on one of the river stones. The sun was setting fast, and I was no closer to finding my important discovery. Not mine, I thought, theirs. Something they could print and claim ownership of in their magazine. To them, it was just another article, another headline, something to stir up the antiquarian community. They dangled my funding and my passion above my head while I scrounged the earth for something meaningful enough, not to me, but to them.

If the roles were reversed, and I was on the board of the journal, I could never think of a reason to refuse an article unless it were false or criminal. This need for fortune and glory would be the end for archaeology, fermented with immoral ethics and greed.

Still, was it wrong to wish for my colleagues' funding revoked instead of my own? I, who squandered all opportunities for nearly a year? They were the ones who were doing the real work and searching out the many mysteries of the ancient world. All I had done was sit about in my library and ridiculed them. Like I had a leg to stand.

"All I'm doing now is sitting on a stone yet again…"

Birds tussled in the canopy, crying out their wiry tones. Finches. I waited for more to fly through the boughs of the Durmast oak tree over my head and spotted their golden feathers high tail it into their nest. I smiled and kicked myself up off the river rock. Reaching down to retrieve the suspected broken tool head, I tossed it in my knapsack, gathered up my shoes, and deduced from the setting sun my way back home.

My wandering hadn't been as far into the woods as I had previously thought, and I soon noticed parts of the path that

I crossed on my journey into the forest. Perhaps twenty or so minutes later, I made it out of the oaks.

The cherry roof of my estate held the last of the setting sun on its face, like a beacon for me to find my way back. The shades of night were starting to overtake the land and I was not hesitant to remain outside for very long. Once inside, I headed straight into my study and put the piece of rock under a magnifying glass. I had to center it into frame, but that was easy enough. The rock itself showed clear signs of knapping on the bladed end. Chipped short and down to give a sharp enough edge for chopping away at branches. There was some wear and tear on the end, likely from Neolithic usage. No plant fibers, but those would have been hard enough to find in a riverbed back in the time of early man anyway. The break in the axe head was near the back. This was where one would take a good branch and tie it around with plant fibers and some tar which I noticed some black residue stuck on the rock.

This wasn't just a rock out in the forest anymore, it was an artifact.

I smiled. A few of the previous discoveries I've made in this forest have suggested the presence of early man. Stone piles, bones of now extinct mammals, even a tooth that was almost too square to be human.

This discovery would confirm my past findings and prove the settlement of early man in Somerset. New excavations, group studies, and research could be made possible by this find! Surely this was good enough for me. It must.

I hastily got out the paper and ink, writing with all of the passion returning to my senses. The thrill of discovery and the new opportunities this would create for the next generation of archaeologists! The presence of early man practically in my backyard! The excitement had returned, or so I thought.

My feverishly written draft reached its final note and the weight of the world returned to my shoulders.

It wasn't until I read over my writings again that all of the confidence and pride which I felt, rapidly vanished. I had been so wrapped up in the excitement of it all, that I forgot to view my discovery through an objective lens. This was a small axe head with no signs of past life nearby, even after I checked my grid multiple times. There were no beings living in this forest. The tool I had found was simply discarded junk at the end of the day. Something this tribe of people used for firewood on their journey somewhere safer.

I had been excited over waste. The journal would not see this as a thrilling find like I had. They'd just see a rock with no brilliance or skill. There was no value in it. I would just be presenting to them a scattered stone.

I wasted another day feeling like my purpose had been decided by someone with a sense of humor.

Chapter 03

There was a knocking on my doorstep which kicked me out of my sleep in the library. I was curled up with *Tess of the d'Urbervilles* by Thomas Hardy when I heard the noise outside. Was it Thursday already? The week had gone by faster than I had anticipated. Christ, my head was aching.

More knocking on the front door beckoned me to my foyer. I unlocked the door and swung it open to find a silver handled cane going in for another knock. It faltered inches from my face, and I leaned back a little late in response. "Oh, Edward. I was afraid that you were out. Does it pain you to open the door in a timely fashion?"

Archie was taller than me with a greying mustache and short chops that held up the buds of cotton on his head. He spoke with no enthusiasm whatsoever, often making for a boring conversationalist, yet there was a charm or swagger his money had brought him in the world of the elite. I had known Archie for seven years after moving into the countryside of Somerset away from the crippling thought bubbles of Oxford or Cambridge Universities. He was a passionate hobbyist for the field of antiquarianism and usually brought all of his finds to my estate for evaluation and sometimes to make a sale. I was wont to purchase artifacts belonging to my ancestor's, but the local museums took awful care of items that did little to bring in large crowds.

I stepped out onto the doorstep to give a hug to one of the maybe four people I would call a friend. "Archie! I'm terribly sorry that I forgot about our teatime today. I've been a little distracted as of late."

He shook his head and smiled. "Not an issue, Edward. I figured as much."

"You figured?"

He paused. "Perhaps we can discuss it further once you've let this weathered old fool in and put on a kettle."

"Of course."

I ushered Archie in through the door, motioned for him to take a seat in the library whilst I rushed off to make the two of us something warm. I chose a robust black tea that I had picked up in Liverpool during a meet with this collector, Irving Braun. Of course, he refused to see any sense in relinquishing his complete set of Byzantine silver necklaces to the recently founded museum in Constantinople. However, my discovery of this tea had been worth the trip.

During my wait, I grew more and more curious of Archie's visit. If I recalled correctly, he wanted me to value an Egyptian scroll which one of his contacts had snagged from an art collector in Zurich. Yet, he arrived with no bags whatsoever. And his assumption of my stress suggested he might be aware of my current standing with the magazine's board despite me not having said a word to anyone on the severity of the situation. Oscar would never have said anything either. He was a tight-lipped editor, most of the board were as well except…

Then, it clicked.

"Eloise told you." I called out in the direction of the library and waited.

Finally, a gruff sigh. "My pupils keep me up to date on all the latest. You know that, Edward."

The kettle sang. I poured half a cup for Archie and a full one for myself, making sure to add plenty of sugar to both. I brought Archie his cup and we sat down comfortably in our chairs. "Thank you, Edward. I was in need of something warm today. I feel the weather changing and you know how the cold makes my bones weak."

"The trees will start to color. I fear we're in for some bad weather this fall."

"Unlike last year."

"Last year was lovely up until the first snowfall."

"That was an awful winter. I'm surprised my roof fared as well as it had."

I took a sip of my tea, the warm, aromatic waters filling my chest with a sprig of cheerfulness. Then, I decided to broach the subject of Archie's visit. "So, I see that you have not brought along that scroll you acquired. Egyptian, correct?"

Archie nodded. "I sent it over to Oxford. I traveled there in June to discuss this semester's plans with Alabaster. He was meeting with some of his students, and I felt the need to give them something real to examine for a change. We can't be stuck reading the same five works all our lives or how do we expect our study to grow?"

"True. Very true."

He drank from his own cup, and I stared out the window into the morning fields of Somerset shaking up from their night's rest. Why is it that the grass always looks divine before and after the night floods the Earth in darkness? Is it the short fear of losing it, or the relief of seeing it still there?

"We need to discuss your… situation, Edward."

Archie grunted to pull my attention, eyes darting between me and the window. We stared out for a second while I remembered how to speak again. "I'm afraid there isn't much to discuss, Arch. Unless I come into finding the most brilliant treasure of our lifetime within the next few weeks, my career is over. They won't publish me again. No one will."

"And have you been tracking down a find? Have you even made an attempt to look into the ancient world? Or have you busied yourself with worrying about losing your dream?"

I shook my head, avoiding my friend's gaze. "It's not easy, Arch."

"I know. You know that I know."

"Yes, well, it's difficult trying to change archaeology when everyone wants it to stay the same. I quit fieldwork because I was sick of seeing these prideful, smug treasure hunters destroying any chance we have of making sense of past civilizations. They bring in dynamite, blow up sites that took men and women decades to construct, and then rob the place of anything that shines. Only half of it ends up in a museum, the ugly half. I'm done with them!"

"Edward, their actions don't have to force your own—"

"But it does, Archie! It does! I went out the other day. Out to the forests. And… and I was so frightened that I might have actually found something. I felt that urge to just take it all for myself. It was just a part of a stone hatchet, but I wanted to keep it. I wanted to run through the whole forest, dig the site down until I could make a bigger find of some kind. Then, claim it all for my own. And… and I was afraid that I would do just that."

Archie laughed heartily. "Edward—"

"No, I'm serious about this. You and the Pemberley's can ask me why I have only written in response to others' finds and discoveries and theories. Well, it's because I'm too damn afraid to go out on my own. Not with how this study is souring. Not with how we are killing our ancestors' work. Not now. Not until it changes."

I quieted down slowly to a horrifyingly low pitch and realized how close I had come to crying my heart out. Archie's laugh waivered, transforming to a friendly smile. "Edward. You are the most careful man I have ever known. You second guess which shoes you put on every morning.

None of your colleagues are as cautious as you and it's a crying shame. However, that doesn't mean we just give up on our dreams. So, what if there are those who make a complete mockery of the field? So, what if they aren't doing any real work, excavating historical landmarks? They are probably the same people who pocket jewelry and ship home entire temples to sit awkwardly in their pleasant estates. You, Edward Davenport, are not one of them. I do not believe it and I won't allow you throwing away your damn life's work this way!"

Archie settled his tea down on its saucer and his eyes reddened until tears worked their way down his cheeks. His hands were shaking, and I feared what he had to say next. "They laughed me out of my dreams, Edward. T-t-those same people made deals behind my back at universities, at museums, even at my own excavations! They pushed me out and… I'm not going to let it happen to you. Your head is too well set on your shoulders. This is your dream!"

I felt a little teary eyed myself and I took another shaky sip from my cup to regain some composure. "Archie—"

"This is not up for debate, my boy."

He spoke sternly, yet with a compassion I was unfamiliar with in my life. His words reverbed throughout my eardrums, slowly forming a static tune in this living room. I could feel his eyes searching over me for any reason to continue his efforts in persuading me.

Perhaps my dreams were misplaced, shattered by an unfit world inhabited with unfit men. Their fires were sparked by old forgotten passions and spent adding more tinder to the flame yet to consume the very earth, our fresh smelling earth, that carried their forms above the starry plane. It was in some of my colleagues' nature to lie and steal. Their pride wouldn't allow them to be made a fool in front of everyone else. These same mortal faults formed the cracks in my field's foundations. The world of archaeology would buckle under their lies, and I could only watch it unfold.

Still, why? Why should I even care for their regrettable actions that would scar our search for past life? Their deeds were their own, their faults would carry them to their graves. Surely my persistence in showing reason before my study would exempt my name from theirs in the history books! My goal should be to provide a well enough example for the next generation of archaeologists on how to better search and preserve our ancestral monuments.

Yet, this is on the assumption that I, myself, will not fall victim to the greed and pride which has afflicted my counterparts. Say I walk onto a site, hair graying if not falling out in clumps, and I find a sparkling gem of emerald in a wonderful Egyptian amulet. A glimmering, dazzling, gleaming green that once touched the heart of an ancient pharaoh or his mistress. Say that I take it, hoard it, lock it away from the rest of the world. Afterall, it is a harmless rock. I like to think that my limited experience has taught me to be better than those galloping over the Alpine mountains in search of fame and wealth. Yet, what if I fail my own expectations?

Though, why? Why get bogged down in the possibilities which have chained me away to my home for days now in fits of anxiety? Why hide my talents away when I have yet to share them with the world? Edward Davenport, you fool! You can't fail yourself with idleness just as you can't fail those born with the same passion and making the same discovery you have now.

Finally, I nodded. I nodded to my own sense as well to my good friend's. Archie smiled over at me and reached into his coat pocket to receive a small slip of paper. "There is a carriage which will be coming to pick you up from your home on the morrow. You will depart for Brighton where you will meet a small group of your colleagues."

Archie stood up from his chair and handed me a short-handed letter. It all felt so sudden, and part of my curiosity wondered whether this was the goal of Archie's meeting all along. Perhaps I would have to pick up a few of those mysteries he's been reading lately to uncover how he has gotten quite so clever in his old age.

He stuck upon his head a velvety top hat and made his way for the door whilst lecturing me. "The team heads for the Aegean. You'll cross the channel and then traverse the continent by train. I know that you get seasick, but I hope the short journey will be bearable."

I stuck the letter in my own pocket and hurried to meet Archie by the door. "You'll make way to the small island of Lesbos. A beautiful Mediterranean gem which I visited once before. They will give you a proper welcome and there are a few temples your team will have the choice of looking over."

Archie opened the door without skipping a beat. "I know it isn't the most exciting sounding adventure, but it was the best I—"

I wrapped my arms around his brittle-boned body and hugged him hard. He nearly croaked before we both shared a caring laugh. When I pulled away, I found myself smiling again. "Thank you, Archie. Thank you for everything."

His cheeks were rosy in the chilling morning air. "Of course, Edward. Just promise me that I get to see what you find first. Before it's published."

I nodded. "We'll have some tea. Maybe I'll even ask the Wilhelm's over."

His eyes widened. "Oh, heaven's no. Not them. Why, did you know the last time I invited them to a party at my estate? Their son, Walther, destroyed my stone wall. Absolutely pummeled it with his carriage."

"Maybe the Hodgkins' instead."

"Yes, I think so."

Archie nodded, smiled, and made way for his carriage

whilst I began to pack my things for my first expedition in

ages.

Chapter 04

Brighton wasn't awfully welcoming on the eve of my arrival. A storm had rolled in from across the seas, tearing down trees and smashing store windows to the dismay of a few disheartened shopkeepers. I had left my estate soon after Archie escaped into his carriage. I was intent on showing up to the town on the night prior to our short voyage across the channel to the continent and sent a message out to town that I wished to depart early.

A kind inn keep had boarded up her cracked windows just as my carriage had arrived in the small coastal town. Wind whipped my coat and flurries of rain made the patchy cobblestone road slippery under my boots. "Scuse me, miss? Is there room in your inn for one more? It will only be one night." I shouted over the thunderous weather.

She put her arms up above her face to help spy my face and, upon noticing baggage and hearing my pleas, she waved me into the doorway. "Let's get ya out of this blooming storm before it tosses the both of us in the drain, shall we?"

I nodded and hobbled with my two bags of luggage into the inn. The owner brushed off her soaking coat, hung it on a nail in the wall, and took her position behind a short counter. She, herself, was not all that tall and peered over the bench just as much as her eyes peered over some spectacles daintily perched on the bridge of her nose. She was a tad older than myself, her face rather handsome, and her smile was only missing a single tooth in the bottom row. "Now, you said one night, is that right?"

I placed my luggage at my feet and took off my short hat out of respect and because it too was soaking wet. "Yes," I cleared my throat. "One night's stay. That'll be all."

She nodded. "That'll be two shillings."

Two? I had expected to pay more than that for a single night's stay and the thought of getting a better deal, although first appearing pleasant, only made me curious of what my quarters would look like. My eyes drifted over my shoulder, leering at the door. The wind rapped against the wooden surface with such ferocity that I feared it would buckle without any notice this night. A cough from the inn keep brought me back to the deal on the table. "Perhaps you'd like to sleep outside. Real cozy, I'm certain."

I shook my head and reached into my coat for my coin purse. Relinquishing two shillings to the owner, she brought me up a flight of stairs to a door at the end of the hallway which reeked like an animal pen. "One night. Breakfast will not be served. You can drop your key off in the morn before ya depart."

She quickly turned her back after handing me the key and speaking her rehearsed speech like a true Shakespearian actor. I was frazzled at her abrupt departure and cautiously examined the room I had spent my own coin on. The door inched open, and my eyes saw what first appeared to be a broom closet, but then I noticed the stained cot on the floor and an oil lamp sitting on a produce box. The smell of animal feces overwhelmed by sinuses, and I had to take a step back to breath the less polluted air in order to regain some composure. Everything about this room was quite awful and I regretted not spending one last night in my estate instead of showing up in Brighton promptly as I had.

I by some means managed to acquire a smidge of rest that night, despite the efforts of the raging storm and the indecent accommodations of my chosen inn. My heart soared at the rising sun, cresting the edge of the coastal village which survived the horrors of an autumn tempest. Men and women and children were all out in the streets to inspect the damage brought on by the nasty weather and I enjoyed watching each of their reactions from the small opening in my room. I refuse to call it a window since a window would require panes of glass which one might be able to see through. This was a shoddy, opaque glaze which was more like a spyglass at certain angles. The approach of morning also entailed a new day and the start of a brave adventure that I was sorely in need of. The coming deadline was soon, and I quickly dressed myself before dropping off my key at the front desk. The inn keep was snoring behind the desk with a half-empty plate of breakfast threatening to fall free from her tired hands. I deftly snagged a piece of bacon from her plate without her knowing and dashed out the door with my luggage while she was still unconscious.

Brighton was a dirty kind of smile. The village itself was mucky with makeshift buildings and plenty of sailor's shouting from the dockyards. However, the people were mostly all beaming with joy. As if the ebb of the modern world was still a distant wave yet to make its mark on their streets. Change would come in due time, but they were simply happy with their community. Smiling, laughing, cheering. The storm from last night did nothing to ruin their insatiable enthusiasm. I even found myself forgetting my own stresses and grinning at the kids playing wildly in the street. Slowly, that faded as I neared the dockyard.

The first sign of modern change appeared on the coast. A row of tall, narrow brick apartments was all lined up facing the water where a long pier stretched out into the channel. At the front of the pier was a kind of tourist attraction with these large oval windows and a domed roof straight from Florence. None of it looked like the village I had just walked out of. This place was one large picture-perfect family vacation photograph, and, in fact, there were a few dozen families already rushing off to the sand with French umbrellas and beach towels. It was clean, new, and probably seemed promising for those families. Yet, after actually spending a night in the real village a few blocks away, this fantasy world felt fake. Nothing but a hollow dreamscape hiding away the true Brighton life behind their columned doorsteps and iron fences.

Some ways away from the beach, the dock was bustling with workers and machines, creating a bit of smog filtering the air. The acrid taste was unpleasant, and I made a point to hurry for the ship which Archie had been kind enough to charter for this expedition. I spotted it lined up near the end with the name on the side *HMS Willa* in white paint. Yet, before I could board, I was blocked by a small crowd of men and women in suits carrying similar luggage to my own. They were all chatting away meaningless banter before the launch. I scanned their faces to see if there was anyone who I might recognize. Most of them seemed to blend together in the end and I just about gave up when I noticed Beatrice Smith, a former university student who I had toured with to the Indus Valley. She had a brilliant head on her shoulders and an infectious enthusiasm for the field which I now envied more than ever.

I walked over to her, bumping into a few crates and workmen on my way. "Beatrice! It's been some time."

Her eyes left their foggy state as she narrowed in on my person. Her smile returned and I felt that enthusiasm grow once again. "Oh, Edward. It has indeed been far too long!" We hugged. "I was just about afraid that I would be on my own for this expedition to Lesbos. Not that I couldn't manage on my own, but—"

"—But it would be nice to have good company." I finished her sentence.

"Of course."

I dropped my luggage at our feet and eyed the watch on my wrist. "Say, shouldn't our ship be ready to launch. I thought we would be leaving at nine."

Beatrice rolled her eyes. "It seems our journey has been put on hold. The person leading our troupe seems to have slept in. I'm not sure how anyone could. We are about to go on the trip of a lifetime! How could anyone sleep without being the least bit restless at the thought of what we might uncover there?”

“Do you know who is taking lead of this expedition?”

“Hmm… I think someone said it was Aldrich or Alan something. I have no idea in the slightest. I jumped on the waiting list at university as soon as I saw the opportunity.”

A squall from the channel brushed up the dockside and a torrent of the looseleaf papers flew out to sea as one poor archaeologist saw all of his studies drift out into the harbor. Beatrice attempted to hold back a smile and I reached out to grab a few of the papers before they were lost to the ocean. The young man walked over to me with sheets of notes tossed under his arms and looked absolutely red with embarrassment. “Thank you, sir.”

I handed him what I managed to salvage. “You must be careful in packing your things, friend. One time, I put a silver pocket watch in my briefcase and forgot to latch it on my trip to Oxford. Damn thing fell out in the carriage."

"How'd you know it fell out in the carriage?" he mindlessly asked whilst arranging his papers.

"Because I saw the driver wearing it on his hip!"

Beatrice smiled and the young man seemed to lighten up a shade. He struck out his hand and I shook it with heart. "Oliver. Oliver Ferguson."

"Edward Davenport."

He paused upon hearing my name. "Edward Davenport. From *Archaeologia*, Edward Davenport?"

I nodded. "And this is Beatrice Smith."

She smiled, although young Oliver seemed too worked up at our meeting to pay the young woman the time of day.

"Sir, I've read all of your articles. Ever."

"So far, you mean."

"Of course," he nodded. "I think your methods are so unique and new to the field. Your notes on Karloff's shipwreck of the Uluburan were beyond critical. It absolutely changed my outlook on the scientific process we take into the field. That's why I packed all of my notes on your articles… Well, why I *had* packed, I suppose."

I felt a bit odd meeting an actual reader of mine, a student who took my ethical critiques to heart. It was both rewarding and awkward at the same time. I felt a new sense of grief knowing that much of my own writing was now sitting at the bottom of Brighton's harbor.

Then, the crowd seemed electrified with newfound spirit. Voices cooed like Romans in the Coliseum at the presence of their favorite gladiator clad in bronze armor. The Nile parted only for one such man. "Adrien Fischer," I mumbled his dreadful name under my breath.

Beatrice seemed a tad shocked whilst Oliver quickly swiveled on his feet to get a glimpse of the Austrian vagabond. The rags-to-riches story was a lie that only few were privy to thanks to a university expedition to Fischer's hometown of Hallstatt. On one night of cheerful frivolity, a drunk fisherman in the local tavern had recognized the self-proclaimed archaeologist and denounced the chap for a braggart noble's son. We laughed and made jokes of Fischer's cleverly detailed stories throughout the whole expedition. He remained silent as the night, upset at being caught in his own spun tale. Ones which I was certain weren't the last.

He was a handsome fellow. Short blonde hair that wisped at the front, a somewhat weak jawline, and glassy green eyes that seemed to follow you wherever you were. When he stood in the crowd of his colleagues, he was in his element. They cheered and applauded him. I smirked and cursed Archie in the wind.

I can only hope this short journey will be bearable.

Christ, I wanted to vomit at the sound of Fischer's voice.

"Let's bring it back together now, friends! The morning is young, and we wouldn't want to bother these dockworkers with your cheering for my arrival!" Adrien's voice was a proud and polished mask.

"Early? We should have left by now…" Beatrice whispered to our small group.

I nodded. "You'll see. The man will twist it into saying that the boat never intended on leaving without him anyway."

"The man's a genius." Oliver spoke, ignoring our small talk.

His eyes were glued to the figurehead of our expedition, drawing a sketch of his eyes in his mind for his next series of notes. I felt sorry for the kid. He had become completely enamored with a façade.

"Now, this is the ship that will be taking us across the channel where we will head by train to Greece and get on another boat to reach Lesbos, a small island where my research suggests we will find a temple to, not one, not two, but three separate deities within meters of each other."

"A temple?" I asked Beatrice.

She shook her head. "A temple with three separate altars side-by-side. One to Zeus, another to Dionysus, and the last to a goddess yet to be named."

"A temple to the almighty Zeus!" he shouted with his arms raised dramatically. The crowd ate his enthusiasm up just like Oliver. "As well as Dionysus, whose famed revelries we will surely share on our trip. And, of course, the renowned mother of gods, Hera."

The crowd seemed more joyful than the usual students I was used to seeing on expeditions and part of me was envious of their blissful happiness.

"I thought you said the third temple was to a goddess none of us were certain of yet?" I whispered to Beatrice.

"We haven't. Adrien Fischer's research suggests it to be Hera despite there being no evidence to suggest she was worshipped there." Beatrice seemed quite peeved at Fischer, and I made the cautious call to keep to myself until after we made it on the ship.

Then, Oliver began to push his way into the crowd and approached Fischer with a handful of papers. "Mr. Fischer! Sir, it is an honor to finally make your acquaintance. Your finds across the continent have sent ripples through the study! It is an honor to be sharing this expedition with someone such as yourself."

Adrien smiled at the whelp, but then his gaze raised to meet my own. We shared a quiet stare, his features unsettlingly flickered with fear before regaining his smile.

"Well. My gods, this is a surprise indeed," his voice full of fake wonderment.

He pushed Oliver and the crowd aside to meet me by the flank of the ship. Beatrice inched out of the way of Fischer's upcoming litany, a wise decision for any person in my position. A second in Adrien Fischer's company was a second wasted.

"Edward Davenport. I was aware that Archie had sent someone to join our voyage, but I figured it was one of his down-and-out students looking to prove themselves. I suppose that I was half right."

Adrien offered his hand, and I shook it like a true gentleman, threateningly hospitable. "Adrien Fischer. I am delighted to join another expedition with someone renowned. However, I believe we might need a bigger boat to fit your ego. Perhaps there has been some mistake?"

We both smiled at one another, waiting for a crack in their character that would excuse one of us from joining this journey. All it would take was a small scrap at the docks, a brawl of savagery as Fischer would no doubt tell the committee, and I would be tossed on my rear end for good. We waited and the crowd grew eerily silent.

"I'm shocked you left your estate. Must be easy to critique others from your home's study. I wonder how real fieldwork will change your opinions on our efforts."

"Not very, I suspect."

He nodded. I wanted to say more, but I knew it would be rather brash to display such animosity toward the lead archaeologist on his own expedition before we had even left the port. I blinked, stepping aside to let Adrien and the group of archaeologists make their way on board. Oliver stopped by my side before heading up. "That's Adrien Fischer! The statue of Solomon! The temple of Asclepius!

This is going to be another stellar adventure for him. I'm certain of it."

I nodded gently and pushed the youth up the stairs to join the rest of Fischer's crowd. Before I headed up myself, Beatrice caught my arm. "Don't be upset, Edward. The man is a total bell end. Let's simply ignore his chatter for the rest of the trip and get some real work done in the meantime."

She smiled brightly and I felt a bit of my spirit restored. I helped her onto the stairs and readied myself on the docks.

This was my last chance to turn back. I knew the trek that was ahead of me. With Adrien Fischer, this might prove to be one of the worst experiences of my career. Someone with little respect for the study was always my nightmare, but Fischer was a different breed of hobbyist. The man enjoyed going on expeditions with experienced archaeologists and attaching his popular name to their work in order to steal the credit when the inevitable article would come out in the journals. A leech and a cretin, I suspected. I feared this might have been the worst outcome, but what choice did I have? If I turned around and headed back to my estate, my work would be over.

The ship's horn blared through the harbor and the seagulls glided overhead towards the modern buildings on the coast. The water was a shade of blue waning green, but the seafoam padded an ugly layer of beige that obscured its jaded surface from my view.

"A test of patience, then?" I laughed for that was all I could really do to reassure myself. I wished Archie would have joined me, but I knew that I needed to do this on my own. So, I gripped the stairs and climbed aboard the shaky ship's rails, my stomach already tumbling in my body.

Chapter 05

The ship was under way within the hour and my gut wrenched with each wave that rocked our watercraft side-to-side. While most of my colleagues chatted with the most humble Adrien Fischer, I sought refuge within the cabin to hopefully keep my mind off of the water surrounding us. During this time, I was introduced to the captain, a young James Whittler, who was a quite robust young man, aged by the tide's toll, yet quickly proved to me that he had an excellent singing voice. Whittler sung thirteen sea shanties, each the wittier than the last, until we reached the shores of France which were fraught with trafficking ships. We made port around mid-day and I thanked James for his hospitality and excellent boatmanship before losing my breakfast of the inn keep's bacon in the harbor. Some snickering ensued from the crowd, yet Beatrice came over to check up on me. She had stayed with the expedition during the journey and was already peeved at Fischer and his lackeys.

"He's a buffoon, Edward. An absolute crowd pleaser. The man was discussing his ventures to the Indus valley, and I asked him of his thoughts on early Sanskrit literature."

I smiled. "Why would you expect such a man as Adrien Fischer to bother reading or listening to native dialects before an expedition?"

She laughed. "He looked at me. He stared right through me with the emptiest expression. I asked him again and he simply talked over me to continue his story for the students."

I stopped Beatrice a few steps back from the crowd and spoke in a hushed manner. "You must understand that not every person who practices archaeology is respectful of the study or its importance. I fear that this expedition will be… trying. On the both of us. Yet, we must hold steadfast if we are to truly uncover hidden truths and better our thinking of the ancient world. So, back straight, head up, and never hold onto the words of men like Fischer who are intent on robbing you of everything that you will accomplish.”

Beatrice nodded, heeding my words and standing up a little straighter afterwards. “I wish you were the one leading this expedition, Edward.”

She headed off to join the group and I took a moment to watch a cluster of seagulls take flight. “You and me both.”

We were slow to leave Le Havre, a town in which I made a note to make a return trip in the future. Everywhere I turned, my eyes were attracted to storefront windows showing off freshly baked breads and desserts, beautiful dresses and suits, and there was even a toy shop busy with young life and imagination inside. Every which way I looked, dozens of people were walking with purpose through the cobbled roads. Streetlamps on every corner. Dogs on leashes. A truly modern city.

We soon reached the station with minutes to spare. The local French gossip, shouts of conductors, and the whistle of approaching trains made for a noisy setting. Yet, it was the life that I enjoyed watching. The mannerisms in which people would speak to one another. Upturned noses, the movement of hands to accentuate their point or denounce another's. A young woman tossed half a bagel in the bin before waving a carriage outside.

A tug on the cuff of my arm signaled that our departure was imminent, and I joined Beatrice in the train car, taking the opportunity to get out my pen and paper from my luggage. If I was to have an excellent article by the time I returned to England, then I would need to set out now before our expedition even bared fruit.

At least, that was the good intentions I had before the first train left the station. There were six in total, taking about a little over three days before we reached the shores of Greece. In that time, I simply took my seat beside Beatrice, retrieved my pen and paper, and stared at its unmarred surface for fear that I might ink the wrong words. Three days and not a single thought occurred on our journey that might inspire my ideas for venturing to Lesbos.

Of course, there was a reason. I knew it, Archie knew it, the whole expedition knew it. I needed to prove my worth in the field of archaeology. That was the issue. There were no words I could breathe onto the page that felt worthy enough of such a monumental task. The fear would always be there, but I had hoped this journey to the continent would assuage some of those worries.

Another thing that made it difficult to come up with any ideas was the sheer stupidity which assaulted the ears in our train car. Adrien Fischer never stopped speaking to the students. The only breath he took was when he took a swig from his pocket flask on the second night. Of course, the liquor only enriched his storytelling abilities and dulled the common sense of everyone around him. There was a point where I had listened to about enough of his ramblings and stood up from my seat. He was encircled by students, also partaking in a bottle of gin they had picked up in Belgrade, who all leaned in with keen interest in Fischer's kind sounding words.

"—and the only person who could fit in this tight little cubby… this antechamber of sorts, was myself. So, they sent me into this hole in the ground with a lantern and a prayer. The walls were cool to the touch, an absolute noiseless tunnel. I peered closer into the antechamber and spotted the shine of gold in these shifting sands. Well, I thought it was sand. But the reality was that the floor was covered in snakes! I didn't realize until I lifted the Byzantine ceremonial dagger up and one tried to crawl across my arm. I damn near bolted back through the tunnel! Shouting 'Close it! Drop the rock! For the love of Christ almighty, drop it!' Absolutely terrifying."

At my approach, Fischer straightened up slightly before offering me a sip from his flask. I shook my head and took a seat near Oliver, who seemed just as drunk as the lead archaeologist and even more engrossed in his story.

"Where was this tomb?" I asked.

Fischer shifted a tad. "In the Parnassus. A small dig with Francis Calloway. You know of Calloway?"

I nodded. "Calloway. The same Calloway who mistakenly found the war helmet of Narses and then forgot to map the area. One of the most famous battlegrounds lost because he was content with the general's helmet. That Francis Calloway?"

Fischer was quiet and the rest of the group eyed their drinks with hesitant looks. Finally, Adrien shrugged and took another swig of his flask. This seemed to make things right with the other students since they followed suit in downing their glasses in following his lead. "We all make mistakes.

That's what we are searching for in archaeology. Any mistakes from the past which might have gone unnoticed. Isn't that right, Edward?"

"Not entirely sure that has anything to do with—" but the man cut me off before I could continue.

"Of course, you'd need to actually attempt something in order to screw it up. Failure is just a part of the equation. We do our best to dredge up what history has tried to steal from us and bring it all back into the world instead of having it rot away in the dirt. Sometimes we are Francis Calloway and can't tell our lefts from our rights." He smiled. "And other times, we're just like I was back in that tomb, and we manage to save a valued artifact."

Oliver nodded along with Fischer's words, like a diligent student at a university lecture. I looked at him differently now than I had at Brighton's docks upon our first meeting. I thought him a bright young lad, carefully mapping out current theories from his betters in an attempt to figure out what kind of archaeologist he would become. Yet now I saw him for what he truly was. None of those papers in his briefcase would matter. All he did was nod and side with the more acclaimed individuals in hopes of ending up in their good graces. My gut knotted up at the sickening realization that all of these students were the same as Oliver and would likely turn out to be the same as Adrien Fischer.

"You pride yourself on your finds, Fischer. Yet, I recall that it was Calloway who wrote the article, and your name was merely attached."

Fischer nodded. "I helped him review our findings. He insisted on writing it himself. Something, you might wish to consider—"

"Findings? You found the shiniest object in a tomb and ran for the hills. You locked the site back down and, if I recall correctly, labelled it 'destitute' of further research."

"Well, after reclaiming—"

"The site has just about been forgotten because of your and Calloway's article. Yet, it sounds to me like you hardly spent any time there. For you would realize that one Byzantine ceremonial dagger would usually come in pairs. You would realize that there were probably three other branches to the antechamber for your team to explore. You would realize that a noble was likely buried there with his family. You, an honored scholar such as yourself, hell, any schooled individual that had spent more than a day on the site would be able to tell this from 'your' find! Which begs the question; how long were you in the Parnassus? Were you even on the site for the duration of the expedition? Or did the snakes scare you off?"

Silence. The train car was quiet for the first time since its departure, and I walked back to my seat with Beatrice in hopes of finding the right words to start my article. Yet, my mind only drew a blank.

When we finally reached Greece, whispers still continued of Fischer and my argument the night prior, which I was quick to inform Beatrice as she had been napping during our little standoff. She found our small spats amusing, though I could hardly share in the fun. If Fischer found my behavior disrespectful or harmful to the expedition, I believe that my last chance to prove myself would be stripped from me by him writing one simple letter to the journal. These little arguments meant little, but I feared that I might push him over the edge on our journey.

Greece was pleasant in the fall. The trees were changing from greens to bright yellows and golds, shedding their colors for the coming winter. The crowds were mostly tourists exploring the ruins of, who they referred to as, their ancestors. Despite their claims, I found it ironic that most spoke German or English.

The ports were slow, and we had to wait nearly an hour before our chartered ship was ready to escort us over to

Lesbos. We were required to have a form of identification as we would be entering the Ottoman's territory. I doubted there would be soldiers waiting for us at the docks, but one must always be careful when travelling to foreign lands. I brushed up on the formal customs and some of the dialects during the boat ride over the glorious Aegean Sea. It, honestly, was one of the most beautiful sights in the world. Crisp, clear water with the lightest hue of blue-green that I could only equate to the city of Athens.

After some hours, we reached the coast of Lesbos and were approaching the docks of Mytilene. The city was neoclassical with orange, brick roofs straight from the Roman empire, spiraling stone towers from the Ottomans, and dirt roads from the poor Greek olive farmers who have seen occupation after occupation. We docked with little resistance from the Ottoman's, although they did ask to see our identification. They waved us in after seeing each of our passports and our expedition finally got started. Many of the students whispered questions as we approached the small, coastal town. When do we get started? Where will be staying? When can we get our spades and break ground?

While their minds were preoccupied with dreams of grand discoveries, I studied each stone structure from the shore to the far reaches of Mytilene. The ones closer to the sea were more Roman in construction with arches and pillars that reminded me of Tuscany than the Greek bay. Yet, the farther one got out into the countryside, the more rugged and ancient the buildings appeared, like they had just been built by Greek hands weeks ago. The people were varied. Some had stronger Greek features while others were soft and tan to which I considered them Ottomans coming here to start a new life. And what a life it must be. To stare out across the Aegean each morning with the smell of Lesbos' forests at your back and farmers wheeling in barrows of fresh olives. The life here was simple compared to London or Paris, but that didn't make it any worse. The modern world hadn't yet claimed Mytilene like it had begun to in Brighton and their easy-going lives brought a hopeful smile to my face.

Beatrice called my name and I hurried back to the group which had stopped outside of a wider brick structure, likely created by the Byzantines. The building was built more for purpose rather than looks and I gathered from hushed voices that this would be the inn where our team would reside for the next few weeks.

While everyone was busy waiting for Adrien to chat up the inn keep, I wandered over to a nearby café where a group of older men were drinking some espressos in short mugs. Upon closer inspection, I realized they weren't all that old. Instead, the callouses on their hands and faces lined with hard labor kept their age a slight mystery. They eyed my approach carefully and one of them even whispered something to their friends. Snickers and smiles.

"Excuse me," I spoke carefully, reminding myself of the local dialect that I studied up on the way here. "Would you happen to know where the Temple of Dionysus is?"

They smiled wider. "Nothing there but dirt, friend." One spoke with a harsh tone that seemed to rein the rest of his posse back to composure. "The temple is further along the coast. Bunch of stones and dirt. Why would you be interested in it anyway?"

I felt nervous from all their uneasy stares. "I'm not interested in it. Yet, my friends wish to take a look around. They have a, how you say, fondness? Appreciation? Appreciation for history and wish to study it."

The rough one of the bunch coughed into his hand and spit a brown drool of tobacco from his lips. "Historians. They've come here before. Found a statue of Zeus, I believe? Then, they left. There is nothing left to find there."

The last words came out with bile and in a threatening manner that made me question if I heard him right. Surely, there must be something left of the temple. The walls might still stand and the article I've read on the site suggests that the temple floor has yet to be broken by anyone skilled enough to recognize rock from tile.

Suddenly, Adrien's voice quieted our chatter. "Edward! What in the world are you doing? Don't waste your time on them. Probably rob you of your coin purse."

"I was simply asking where the Temple of Dionysus could be found."

"Yes," Adrien smiled. "Likely these men have been there. Likely they've already looted it of simple treasures and figurines. Again, I must ask, why waste your time on liars and thieves?"

The men clearly were uncomfortable at Adrien's speech. Perhaps they had picked up a few of his words and were unsettled by his tone. They returned to their espressos and pretended to ignore us, save for the rough-looking one. He eyed me with a stare that felt like a pistol was being waved in my face.

I shook my head. Adrien grabbed me by the shoulder and helped me find my way back to the inn. The men looked between one another before getting up to return to their families.

Chapter 06

We spent the rest of the day exploring Mytilene. Fischer and most of the men headed out to the local tavern to try out the famed liquor, ouzo, as it was a native delicacy. I believe he just wanted to deepen his cups and tell some more tall tales to inspire our group. There was never a dull look on any of the students and for that reason alone, I appreciated Adrien Fischer's optimism. Yet, his methods were another story.

Beatrice and Oliver, reluctantly, joined me on a short trip to the Castle of Mytilene. Big blocks of stone made an imposing wall standing tall along the Mytilene coast. I had read of its history, its construction starting sometime in the Justinian era of the Byzantines, the fort was built on the shoulders of Ancient Greek structures that no archaeologists had yet to identify. The fort itself was mentioned in a few of Homer's own works. To gaze upon the same walls that once were new to the ancient world was extraordinary but also melancholic.

They were in shambles, breaking under age, the temper of angry gods, and neglect. The shuffling of empires no doubt hindered its repairs and I wondered how the men and women who built this fort would feel now knowing its current state. Would they be proud that their walls still stand or saddened that it was forgotten by those it was meant to protect?

"Why are we not excavating here?" I suddenly asked. We had left the main keep and were walking the shoreline in the rhythm of the waves.

"Well, Adrien Fischer believes there is something to be learned elsewhere on this island—" Oliver started before I cut him off.

"Yes. I know what Adrien thinks he knows. But… there is history here. There is life right outside its gates. Surely the likelihood of discovering something would prove better closer to the city of Mytilene than out in the forests."

"What? In this fortress? It was constructed by the Byzantines to control the Aegean. Wouldn't we find something more intriguing at the Greek temple?"

I was about to chime in, but Beatrice answered for me. "This land existed before the Byzantines, Oliver. Its people have lived here for centuries. The Byzantines would have built on top of constructed roads and past works. They owed nothing to the Greeks. Perhaps Edward is right about this one."

Oliver scoffed to himself, but I could hear him clearly. "Yes, and the Greeks worshipped their gods. In temples. Like the one we will be digging. There isn't anything we don't know from that castle."

His words sounded borrowed from Fischer and the pit in my stomach since before our voyage grew far more unpleasant.

Our walk ended soon after and we returned to the inn for a good night's rest before we set out at dawn's break to lay eyes on our site for the first time. Although the castle remained in the back of my mind, it was still exhilarating to lay eyes on an ancient Greek temple.

We rode on horseback across the forested island to the western coast where we were told the temple remained. In an hour's time, we reached our dig site.

To the uneducated eye, perhaps one would make the assumption that it was a pile of rubble. Nothing more than a few dozen broken pillars and a foundation of cracked stone that held no semblance of life besides the sprouting of weeds. To my colleagues, it might have appeared disappointingly small and insignificant. Yet, I was ecstatic.

The temple was absolutely Ionic with its ram horn shaped volutes and expertly carved fluted pillars. There was no color left on its surface, simply white marble. Still, one could see the chisel marks marginally tempering its perfect surface. To achieve such a perfect décor was nearly impossible, let alone surviving centuries onward. The base was strong, sturdy, and built facing out over the Aegean. I imagined standing in the temple after it was built by Greek hands and smelling the wine and breads on the altar for the three gods. Dionysus would have brought a loud and cheerful lot, so I pictured the voices of his followers making merry out in front of the temple. Looking across the bay, the wind pulled the vast canvas of trireme sails forth to open water. Carrying the colorful insignia of the Athenians or the Spartans or whichever home they proudly raised their flags to; the ancient world was alive with a vivacious spirit.

And still, I too was disappointed like my colleagues. For I could tell right away that the temple had been looted. Just from looking over the tossed stone piles and the tools strewn about the site from lazy archaeologists in the past or possible looters, I knew that we would find very little here to warrant an outstanding discovery.

Beatrice noticed my head hanging low, but she had yet to realize how fruitless our expedition would be from a single glance at the temple floor. "What a mess!" She commented furiously.

The horses and our group gathered around the entrance to the temple and Adrien Fischer stepped off his steed, taking a mockingly heroic stance. "This site holds potential. We may not see it. It might be buried deep within this rubble. But I promise you all, it is here. Today, we break ground. And possibly unearth some of the greatest secrets history has to offer the modern world!"

Everyone cheered and were quick to dismount their horses. Smiles, bright eyes, true ambition and the thrill for adventure. I stayed upon my horse, refusing to disembark right away. "Adrien," I waved him over.

Fischer already had his papers out and was directing students to each corner of the temple for excavation. His name was rotten, yet pure gold to his own ears. Adrien's head swiveled, noticed my attention, and finished his orders before approaching me. "What is it, Edward? I was thinking you could look out over the north side while I handled the south."

"What in the world are you doing?"

He froze. My tone was biting and clearly caught him off guard. "What do you mean what am I doing?"

"You are sending them out to dig without surveying the site! We have no idea what we are looking at right now!"

Adrien waved a paper in front of me. "I've got a map from the previous expedition right here!"

"From '89?"

"Whitlock and Stromm. The first and only expedition in Mytilene. What's the problem?"

I grabbed the site map from his hands and waved it around in my balled fist. "This site map was over a decade ago! We have no idea what the erosion from being on the shoreline has done to the foundation nor if anything has been misplaced by looters! We can't start without a clear understanding of what we are getting into!"

"Nothing has changed! I've studied the site map and read the original expedition notes, so don't play the *holier than thou* speech to me. We need to start today if we are ever to reach the goals I have outlined for our team."

"Fischer, this site has absolutely changed!" I stared at the site map he had offered me and was surprised to find that the rubble in the center of the temple floor was missing from the first expedition. "We have to record this. Not only for our own digging, but also for future archaeologists."

A crowd was starting to form, and I realized their presence much sooner than Fischer since his back was still turned to the students. Fischer's face drew inward to a reddening snarl and his voice became ragged. "I allow you to come onto my expedition out of respect for our common friend, but I will not listen to you speak of ethical practices when you haven't braved an adventure to a real antiquity site in years. Years! You've never put your work on the line, your name, your credibility. You hide away and judge those around you in the field that you are too frightened to face. I allowed you here! So, don't twist my words in front of my team. Don't fill their heads with doubt and worry or else this study will never get off the ground. You will dig your quadrant with your group, make a pitiful discovery that won't matter in a decade, and then write an article to save your name. Do that, or don't. I don't care what you do. Just stop pestering my team!"

A crescendo quieted down to mere whispers before the temple grew silent as the grave once more. Students looked on with wide eyes and Fischer soon turned around to see his audience before him. He simply shook his head and waved everyone back to work as if our argument was natural for every archaeological dig. I feared it would set a bad example, but there wasn't much I could do now. I had overstepped much too early in this venture.

Oliver walked over to me while Fischer was watching over Beatrice's group. He offered his own advice on how I might better rectify my transgressions towards Adrien in hopes of adding my name to his published article. Honestly, I drowned the kid's voice out after he mentioned Adrien's name like it were our late beloved Queen's.

I waited for Oliver to leave before taking my seat in the dirt on the north side of the temple grounds. There wasn't much on this end of the temple of interest beside a walking path that led back to the dirt road our troupe rode in on. The two teams I oversaw soon grabbed their tools up from the knapsacks on their horses and broke ground within ten minutes of arriving at the temple. I took the liberty of grabbing my notebook and started to jot down every little feature I could make out from where I was seated with utmost diligence. Along with the thrill of discovery and the vigor of youth, the students would make short work of the dig site. Whatever I couldn't describe, I drew with my pencil on the next page.

Stone foundations, three in total. One large. Approximately seven by five meters. Grass climbed through the gaps of forgotten Greek masonry. Three pillars remain. Ionic. About twenty centimeters tall.

The second foundation was faded into the Earth. The stones had come undone in the years since the last excavation. All that remained was a pile of rubble thrown on top of the soil. Likely dug up by looters in hopes of finding a statue for worldly gain. No pillars, though there was a chunk of marble likely from a slab that had come free from the original.

The third foundation was most interesting, and I was proud to see it on my side of the site line so that Fischer might not muck up its contents. It was the most intact of the three, although there were no distinguishing marks on its surface to suggest it was a part of the temple. No names or glyphs on any of the five pillars of marble, still perfectly filleted with Ionic volutes at the base. This was probably the reason why it had been left untouched by looters. That or…

I stared closer at the foundation and found flowers set aside by where an altar once stood. They were purple horseshoe orchids. A light blue ribbon was wrapped loosely around their verdant stems. It was then that I realized how pristine this site was in comparison to the other temples. The grass was clipped neatly, and the stones were free of weeds. The marbles were polished and perfectly preserved from its one-meter height. And the flowers…

A thought came to mind, but I dashed it free as soon as it entered. There was speculation and then there was theory. I would not let my mind stagnate over the former.

The rest of the day was agonizing for me. Standing aside while inexperienced students ripped free dirt and stone from the antiquity site; it was almost painful. To see any chance of understanding the ancient world crudely dashed by the next generation of historians, that was heartbreaking. Yet, the worst part of it all was that I could do nothing about it while Fischer ordered them to rip apart this beautiful site. Just for more fame. Just for glory.

I knew at that moment that I would never step foot on the

temple floor going forward. There was no point in

muddying up the waters any more than they already have.

Chapter 07

We returned to Mytilene's nameless inn, a true brick-in-the-wall kind of place, and I spent the night revising my notes and making sure that at least some documentation of the site's current condition was being recorded by someone. The next day was full of promise. The sun rose slowly with its colorful allure over the bright blue Aegean. I snuck out of the inn early in hopes of getting a better sense of the life surrounding this small coastal town. I walked down the main road, enchanted by the delicious smells wafting out of the bakery. Along the way, I watched three Ottoman sailors enter a barber shop where one of their friends was getting their beard trimmed. A small paper boy was racing in between townsfolk with the public news in his small hands. He shouted his normal tune in hopes someone might actually toss him a coin or two for his efforts. Or simply to shut him up.

He came up to me now that I was approaching and tried to barter with me in Greek. I pulled on my empty pockets, and this seemed to get the message through to the boy since he raced past me to pester the next person in the street.

It was so peaceful. Completely opposite of the modern world that was slowly encroaching toward the British Isles. There was a simplicity to the way of life. Money wasn't at the forefront of everyone's minds. No. Each of them lived slow lives. They were too busy with ordinary life to worry about material wealth. They had no concerns, and I was almost envious of the lives I saw jauntily walking over to the seaside café and ordering a morning coffee with no intention of leaving the table until late in the afternoon. Some of the men at the café I recognized from my first day here in Lesbos. They were the workers who had threatened us not to study the temple grounds. They had yet to notice me walking the street and I decided to go introduce myself to them with hopes of a better outcome.

"Excuse me, friends. Might I join you for some coffee?"

They turned at the sound of my voice and the rougher sounding one was quick to recognize me. His friends were shocked at my walking over to them, almost like I had challenged them in some way. Yet, the talker of their group simply nodded his head, and I took a seat beside him. His friends were still a tad shifty at my joining their ranks, but the big guy didn't mind it much. In fact, he seemed almost amused by my return to their fold.

"Where's the curly haired one?" he asked, and I assumed he was referring to Adrien.

"He likes his sleep," I joked.

The men seemed to find it almost funny, snickering lightly between sips of their coffees. "And you?"

I shook my head. "I can't imagine missing the… sunrise." I forgot the word for sunrise and pointed across the bay at the bright yellow star to hopefully get my point across.

They each nodded and I assumed they understood me fine.

A young waiter arrived at our table and brought me a mug

of coffee with a dash of cream and sugar, the Venetian style

as it were, and hurried off to attend to other customers.

Most of them were older in age, a few couples. Our seats

were a distance away from the rest of the crowd, and I

gathered from their posture that these men frequented this

café on the usual. Likely before each workday.

A meaty hand reached out to seek my own. "Jayson," he

said proudly.

I shook his hand. "Edward."

He waved his hands across his friends and spoke slowly so

that I might understand him better. "We are Ottoman

refugees. We work the olive farms outside of the city. I see

many travelers walk past the temple every day. They don't

like you digging the grounds up."

"Neither do I."

"Can't be much left to find there. Men like the malaka you were with stole everything already."

I assumed he was referring to Adrien and simply nodded to show some understanding to this man and his friends. "You were right to be worried of us. Men like Fischer, the malaka, don't care about much of anything. They just want the wealth or fame which the discovery of foreign treasures brings to graverobbers in modern society."

He paused. "Are you not one of them? Did you not come here to steal from this place too?"

His friends eyed me, and I felt more unwelcomed than I did when I first arrived in Mytilene. There was no point in lying to them. I was here for something. Wasn't I? I needed to prove my worth and that meant robbing these people and the locals of Lesbos of their history. Was I no better than Fischer? Then those I scolded in my papers?

Of course, I wasn't like them! I, unlike him, was in this search for the sake of my career as opposed to his needless reckless behavior. And I had abstained from the digging up of the site. My methods were more cautious, and I wanted to believe that counted towards something in the hearts of these men.

Their stares proved otherwise. I could only sit there like an absolute fool and sip my coffee until they each got up to leave to prepare for an arduous day in the olive forests.

Soon enough, my colleagues awoke from their rest, Fischer being the last one to exit his room, and we were able to gear up our horses. Whilst riding the dirt path to the temple, Beatrice pulled her horse alongside my own at the back of the group and we spoke together in hushed tones so as to not be overheard by the rest.

"He tore a quarter of the foundation for the Dionysus alter out of the Earth yesterday."

"Fischer?" I was astounded.

"No, Oliver. Fischer told him to do it. He wanted to compare the context of the rock to the cliff face."

"That's absurd! They would have taken the rocks from a quarry up the hill before carrying chunks of heavy rock up the beaches."

"That's what I said. He didn't listen."

I shook my head. Beatrice's horse whinnied with excitement as we drew closer to the temple grounds, and she readied to get back to the group before our arrival. As she rode on, she spoke mockingly to her greying horse. "The modern archaeologist only needs two things to be successful. Luck and a room full of morons who'll listen."

I pulled back on the reins to let the group go ahead of me. A numbing migraine was starting to form at the base of my skull and work its way through my synapses to my pain receptors. I feared that Beatrice was right. That the standard of archaeology would cascade back into the days of antiquarians where the wealthy would rob and kill indigenous tribes for anything that shined in their rivers. Perhaps, it would be worse than that. They wouldn't even discover anything new. They would simply make claims with no finds, no evidence, no context. Only to present a history made up of lies.

My hand instinctively reached up to my forehead to brace some of the aches from my migraine as well as block out the rising sun climbing the cliff face in line with the temple's altar of Zeus. Fischer was already delivering a quick speech for our crew, and I leisurely hobbled over to my seat in the grass that I had taken yesterday. He spoke of our 'importance' and threw out words like 'righteous duties' and the 'preservation of our ancestors.' It was all a bit pretentious sounding, but the kids liked the man's powerful voice and, most likely, they wanted the same fame that he possessed.

If only they knew the truth. Of the illusion Fischer liked to project upon himself. Maybe they'd see how wrong his methods were. Or, perhaps, they just wouldn't care at all.

As he sent the students back out to their assigned site quadrants for more digging, my eyes returned to the preserved altar. I found myself holding my breath at the sight of flowers bound up in ribbon sitting idly in the center. They weren't the same purple horseshoe orchids from yesterday.

No, these were rainbow orchids. Quite similar in design with their curved petals that liked to droop on the flowers stem. Yet, unlike the purple horseshoe, the rainbow orchids had folds of yellow that slowly evaporated into the same deep purple as the horseshoe. I was almost astounded that I had noticed such a slight difference in flower. The ribbon was still the same baby blue as yesterday, but it was nearly identical to the other small bouquet.

Even so, my doubtful mind had to question my instincts. For what if they were the same? Perhaps I had made an error. I sighed. What if I had misidentified the flowers before, not noticing their tint of sunflower yellow in the midst of our excavation? It was a such an easy thing to mistake two orchids for being the same. Surely, I must be wrong. I mean, what were the odds that anyone could possibly be placing these flowers at this altar on the regular. It was most peculiar, and I needed to rest my mind by taking a walk around the temple grounds. At least, I had hoped to calm my restless thoughts.

It was a purple horseshoe. It had to be. These were different flowers. Right?

I strolled over to the cliff and looked out over the blue Aegean as I had with the Ottoman olive farmers earlier this morning. The shared sight held more light than the early morning and I enjoyed how crystalline the waters seemed at this hour. Almost like looking through a cascading gem or diamond.

No. I had made an error. Why would anyone place flowers at a forgotten temple? What was the purpose?

I was jealous of this island and its beauty. It owned this view, the locals shared it, and we were simply visitors. Yet, that didn't lessen the fact that I wished to wake up to such a sight every morning myself. A short red-backed squirrel scurried up an olive tree with the island's precious small fruit in his protruding cheeks.

And what if someone did bring the flowers here? Who were they? What significance did this unnamed temple altar have for that person? And why not place flowers on the altars for Dionysus and Zeus?

Suddenly, I felt a pat on my shoulder and the shock of Adrien by my side made me shudder out of my own thoughts. He took a ridiculous stance beside me, an attempt to make himself look daring on the edge of the cliff and let out an almost giddy sigh. "We're getting close to finding something already. I can feel it, Edward. Something that will surprise the entire field, I'm sure."

A crisp wind surfed up the side of the rocky cliff face with salty sea air threatening to knock us off our feet. Fischer stumbled a little, but I breathed in the fresh air in hopes of rejuvenating my spirits. It worked phenomenally well, and I almost forgot Adrien, or my other colleagues, were even present at the temple grounds. I could feel it, that discovery Fischer mentioned. It was not only in the Earth that the Greeks once worshipped, but also in the same air I was breathing. I imagined them staring out across the stretch of sea that belonged to Poseidon, a beautiful gift for man. I reached down and grabbed up the pebbles that had come free from Gaia's hold on Lesbos. Sharp fragments of limestone that were cooled by the winds. I realized why this temple had been placed here. It wasn't only a place of worship for the ancient world. It was peace. It was freedom.

It was the closest one could get to those who guided them.

I let out a deep breath and was returned to the dig site and Adrien Fischer was still helplessly trying to stand upright in the abrasive winds. We took a few steps back from the cliff face. "I believe we have already discovered something."

My words were outed before my mind could understand how they would be perceived by Fischer. Of course, his materialist nature instantly kicked in. His face was full of surprise, and he rushed around my side to face me directly with a desire to know more.

"What have you found? A statue? An urn? What?"

I tilted my head over to my side of the temple, at the purple flowers. His face fell, drooping with disappointment. "I-I— I don't see anything. What did you find?"

I shook my head with frustration and walked him over to the altar site, some of the students' stares shadowed the two of us as they lost interest in their own work. I knelt down over the pristine temple ground beside the rainbow orchids and Fischer seemed to copy my own movements. He waited for an explanation, and I just stared at the marbles with a new perspective on our expedition.

Finally in an impatient huff, Fischer expressed his frustration. "What are you telling me right now? That you've gone and picked some flowers! This is absolutely asinine! I thought bringing you along for this journey would prove you a valuable asset. Now, I realize the truth. You have lost your mind! The journal is going to love hearing about this."

I shushed his mindless chatter and carefully put my hand to the marble surface of the temple floor. "Do you not see this?"

"What are you on about, man?"

I raised my hand up to face both of us and smiled. It was perfectly clean. And when I say that I don't mean there was some dirt or clay on the edges of the altar floor. No, it was bone dry marble. Perfectly fresh white rock.

"It's clean," I clarified.

Fischer seemed ready to blow a gasket and I hurried my theory along to stop his face from turning beet red.

"You can see from the brush strokes on the surface of the temple floor that this one, unlike those of Zeus and Dionysus, has been kept clean of dirt and rock. It has been maintained by the locals. Likely, this has been going on for centuries. Do you see it now?"

Fischer slowly caught on, but his lips curved into a frown. "What are you trying to insinuate here, Edward? That the people of Lesbos still worship their gods? I felt like that was a given."

"No. No. No. But don't you find it curious that it is this altar. Surely, the god of gods, Zeus, would be honored. Hell, even Dionysus is well known in myth around Lesbos. But do you see any symbols here? Any names? And yet, this one is the altar that they chose to maintain. Why?"

"Why?" Fischer grew upset. "Why do we even care? What the people do now has nothing to do with what we are trying—"

"It has everything to do with it!" I cut Fischer off before he headed down that road of thought. "The daily lives of these people have hardly changed since this temple's construction. If they are maintaining it, then, perhaps it is possible that they still worship this altar. The question is—"

"What does it matter? If you consider they're offering up those purple flowers there, then let me show you something."

Fischer stomped off across the temple grounds and I followed in pursuit of his logic. A few of the students also carried on after us to see whether a fist fight would break out as it almost had yesterday. Adrien stopped atop the hill opposite of the temple and waved his hand with all the showmanship he possessed to persuade me.

Across the way was a white-painted Catholic church with its front facing the dirt road. The shingles on the roof had come mostly undone, likely from the raging ocean air. There was a bronze cross situated in the ground beside the structure and a handful of nuns along with a heavy, aged priest were reading out psalms from their black-covered Bibles. At their feet, a spread of purple orchids was growing out of a flower bed around the bronze cross.

"Purple flowers. As purple as the papacy. I reckon one of the nuns or all of them like to walk the dirt road and read their stories out to the locals as the Romans no doubt did when they ruled this island."

Fischer, feeling justly smug, headed back to the temple grounds and continued to instruct others what to do. I stood there, watching the crowd of nuns finish their religious meeting before returning to my side of the dig site. The remainder of my day was spent watching over the students test which hammers were best at breaking marble slabs.

Chapter 08

The second day ended similarly to the first, with me writing up my notes throughout the night whilst listening to the joyous laughter of my colleagues at the local tavern. I paused in my writing when I reached the point where I was explaining my theory of the altar site I had been assigned to by Fischer. Returning to the scene of our recent argument brought back all of the emotion running through this expedition. So much was on the line and yet I still felt like I was waiting for my great discovery to walk itself into my hands. Sitting in the dirt would not bring anything new and neither would digging up a site that had clearly been looted long ago. Which brings me to the only conclusion that one can make in my position. I needed to discover whose deity was being worshipped at the pristine altar.

It was labeled impossible by the previous expedition since this part of the temple grounds had no markings whatsoever to identify any past rituals. Those secrets had long been erased, whether by erosion or looters. Still, there was one route left to be pursued by my predecessors.

The flowers.

I knew they were the key to my discovery. The only thing I theorized was left to learn from this site was the identity of whose altar was still being maintained by the people of Lesbos. Everything else on this expedition became irrelevant to my own search and I focused in on what I knew about the altar.

Besides still being kept clean and worshipped by the locals, there wasn't much else to go on. The stones had been sheared of all markings there. There were no names, glyphs, or symbols which might point me in any direction. Honestly, besides knowing that this part of the temple grounds once was an altar of worship from previous excavations, there would be no identifying markers to demonstrate its past function in society. Yet, it was the most intact of the three other altars since the stones were in better condition and even some of the altarpiece remained.

The two other altars might be a lead that I could follow. After all, wasn't it interesting that Zeus' and Dionysus' altars were left in disrepair?

The previous archaeologists who worked on these temple grounds had often described the third altar as the one most likely designed for Hera, the mother goddess. Perhaps those before had also found the purple flowers and were drawn to that conclusion. It wouldn't be a stretch of the imagination to assume that Hera and Zeus would have shared temples since they often were worshipped closely. Yet still, a part of me couldn't believe that the altar for Hera would have been stripped of all titles and symbols.

That was the part I was having difficulty with. Why would anyone chip off the names on an altar? What could have caused such an action and, if it were the locals, why were they still worshipping there?

My mind was left twisted in knots as I shut my oil lamp and headed to bed. I remember dreaming of flying. It felt like I was swimming in the middle of the ocean with no sense of direction. I kept flying circles over Mount Etna yet could not figure out how to land atop its peak.

When I awoke, it was late in the morning, and I cursed myself for sleeping in. I hurried putting myself together in some work boots, rough cut pants, and a flannel shirt. It was a bit chilly out and I grabbed up a warm winter coat from my luggage before rushing out the inn door. To my disappointment, the olive farmers had already left the local cafe to work the forests and I had to sit at the table with my steaming coffee alone until my colleagues were ready for the day.

As expected, Adrien Fischer was the last one to leave his room. I had managed to finish two cups of coffee by the sea before being called out to by Beatrice that it was time to set off on our horses again. We chatted about the change in weather this morning and prayed that we would return to a more temperate setting later in the week. We also discussed my argument with Fischer, although it was Beatrice who dredged up that sour topic, almost infatuated now with this mysterious third altar. Then, she detailed some of the names I was being called by the other students on the trip, to which some I found quite amusing. They had clearly fallen victim to Fischer's delusions, and I found it laughable how wrong they were.

Of course, this didn't mean I wasn't offended by their stories. I had no issue with them making fun of my cautious nature, but it was frightening to see how easily their thinking gave way to Fischer's foolish methods. They were all completely fine with destroying antiquity sites that have been standing for centuries so long as their names were connected to a famous discovery.

I feared that my worries for the modern archaeologist were coming to fruition, and I was silent the rest of the ride to the temple grounds.

It was another day of destroying history. The ripping up of stone foundations was furthered by the instrumental Adrien Fischer who believed our expedition would find earlier works yet unearthed by looters if we plowed through the temple floor. I took notes on their destruction of the grounds in hopes of creating a map for future teams to delineate what we added… or rather, removed in our searches. Besides the usual harm done by our inexperienced youths and frustratingly ignorant lead archaeologists, it was a rather average day at the dig site.

I hated the idea of this becoming the norm, however. The idea that each day we came down to this temple would mean further deterioration of the surviving structure. It was something horrifyingly depressing to witness. Was there no other outcome? Could we not have observed the site and drawn conclusions first before having to tear its glorious marbles apart?

It was only the third dig day and I found myself despising my colleagues. I needed to get away from them, so I came up with a clever solution to my problems.

As the auburn sun started to set across the Aegean and our troupe were setting off on our horses, I held back at the temple. Adrien noticed my apprehension to leave and dismounted his steed.

"Edward, we are all heading back to town to get something to quench our thirst. You can join us if you like?" His words felt genuine, as if he had already dulled his memory with enough alcohol the other night to forget our past grievances.

I shook my head. "I think I might stay here a while. The quiet might help me jog some ideas. Besides, who can beat a view like that!" And I gestured over to the cliff where dusk brought an array of sapphiric blues and ruby reds intermingling with the promise of night.

Fischer nodded, perhaps a bit saddened that I hadn't accepted his offer and left on his horse back to Mytilene. I waited until the last of them had left until I started to forge a proper plan.

Today's trip had changed everything. Today, I knew for a fact that someone was leaving flowers at the altar every day. To confirm my findings, I examined the third altar upon my arrival and was pleasantly surprised to find that the flowers had returned to purple horseshoe orchids and thus became the catalyst for my actions right now.

I planned on waiting by the dig site, throughout the entire night if that's what it takes, in order to learn the identity of the person who still leaves offerings for the god whose name has been stricken from the temple. If they were leaving offerings, then that must mean that they know which deity this altar belongs to and that, in my opinion, would make for a worthy article. Surely the *Archaeologia* would have to accept that! As well as cure my inveterate headache…

So, with the darkness of the hour setting in, I took up position beside one of the surviving marble pillars by the altar of Zeus. It put me in front of the cliff face, providing a stunning view with the blanket of stars now reflected in the Aegean waters, as well as placed me in close enough proximity to ascertain the person's face in the shadows.

The position wasn't the most comfortable, as I soon found out within the first hour, and I wished that I had chosen a spot in one of the nearby olive trees that overhung the dirt road. Yet, I was too stubborn to change my position now and I settled in for a long night.

Hours came and went. The night brought a darkness unknown to those lucky to live in London whose streets were brightened with tall lamps that never dimmed. Yet, it felt almost peaceful. There were no oppressive swarms of black flies like in Sommerset and the air was cool, if maybe a drab cold. And I felt the urge to shut my eyelids and breathe in the fresh night air that coddled me like a babe.

Just then, a rustle on the dirt path brought me and my senses to the forefront of my surroundings. I remained as still as possible so as to not be spotted right away. More footsteps sounded from the dirt path. Suddenly, I was aware that there was more than one person coming to the altar site by the conversation between two women in Greek. They were whispering and I couldn't make much from their dialogue. Still, I had only anticipated one person worshipping this altar and I dared a peek from behind my stone pillar to spy how many more followers this deity had found on Lesbos. Encircling the altar were at least a dozen robed figures, each carrying a purple flower in their hands.

I seemed to have stumbled across some nightly ceremony and chose to keep my presence unknown to these strangers for the time being. Their whispering stopped as a hunched figure stepped free from the crowd and collected the flowers from the hands of each follower. Then, carefully, they tied the flowers together in a similar blue ribbon that had been used before and nestled the bouquet at the base of the altar floor.

Then, a quiet prayer passed through their lips and each one of them pulled back the hood of their robes to reveal long locks of golden or onyx hair fall back over their shoulders. Their faces were illuminated by moonlight, revealing their sect to be made up entirely of women. The aged figure who seemingly led the group possessed a nest of grey split ends and a wry smile. Then, each of them started to chat about nothing in particular. They were a merry crowd and I felt slightly ashamed of myself for watching on unbeknownst to their group.

Finally, I decided to break free from the shadows and stretch my aching legs from their slumber. With a bit of a hobble, I stood up from my seat and firmly announced myself.

"Pardon my intrusion, but I was wondering if one of you might be of some help to my research."

The chatter and giggling came to an end as they all turned on me with upset looks of distress and worry. Neither of them returned a word to me and the night air that once felt like a pleasant blanket became a kind of noose around my neck. I assumed by their silence that my mere presence seemed to break one of their cardinal rules. None of them tried to apprehend me, but simply waited for one of their sisters to decide what to do with me.

A tall woman with a sharp chin line, soft cheekbones, and hazy green eyes took a step forward in front of the older woman in a most protective manner. She possessed curly, brown hair and short lobed ears that stuck out slightly. She refused to say a single word to me. All she did was gesture to her group a nod back toward the dirt path and they each understood that now was their time to leave the temple.

The rest of her gathering headed back up the dirt road past the Catholic church, redonning their short hoods to hide their features. The aged woman and the brunette remained at the altar. I felt terribly out of sorts for disrupting their ceremony. My shoulders felt heavy, and I frowned.

"I'm sorry. I didn't mean to disrupt your nightly ritual. You see, I am a part of the team of historians studying this ground and—"

"Your team has ruined our temple." Her voice was low and venomous.

I nodded. "You're right. It's wrong. All of it. None of us had any right to step foot on your grounds."

This seemed to catch her off guard and I noticed the old woman behind her had now stepped to the side to get a better look at me, the interloper. Her smile had been stricken from her aged face, but it had been replaced with curiosity instead of hostility.

"They come here looking for treasure," I joked. "They think they are doing the right thing. That they will get famous for finding something of significance, something valuable. It's all just to feed their egos and desire for adventure. I think that you are wise to not trust any of them."

"And you?" She turned her nose up at me. "You are the same as them. You come here each day and stand aside while they rip up our temple. Now, you've hidden yourself away to… what? Learn our secrets? Reveal us to the world? Steal our treasures?" She laughed. "All of our valuables have been taken by men like you."

I wasn't sure if the air had always been bitter or only after she spoke, but I found it impossible to speak another word. For she was right. I had been complicit in my colleagues' destruction of this site. I had failed the people of Lesbos by letting men like Fischer destroy their heritage. I was just as much at fault.

While I tried to find the right words, the woman turned aside and helped walk the old lady back up the dirt road. Every once in a while, the old woman would turn around to check on me. With no more reason left to stay at the dig site, I grabbed up what remained of my pride and hurried off to the inn with hopes of getting some sleep before tomorrow.

Chapter 09

Last night's restless sleep proved useful only in waking me up early enough to head down to Mytilene's café before the olive farmers left for work. They had each just been waited on by the café workers and I hastily put in an order for an espresso before taking my seat at their table. Surprisingly, I no longer received any of the stares from their crew nor felt the awkward air I had perceived on my initial introduction. We drank our drinks when they arrived and chatted about simple things. Jayson was quite intrigued by this one play that he had experienced in a theatre while he visited London with his wife. It wasn't until after he described some of the story that I was able to determine that he was talking about *The Cruel Kindness*, written by Catherine Crowe. We talked about its colorful poesy, and it wasn't until I mentioned that the play had been written by a woman that he was seriously taken aback.

"Was it actually?" he inquired with genuine surprise.

I nodded. "It's rare for a woman playwright to get her work to stage, let alone be critically acclaimed by the public."

"Shame. That play was quite good."

"Indeed."

We sipped our coffees and Jayson's group of olive farmers soon scattered off to work the forests once more. I was left waiting at the café with my head full of nonsense. Well, that wasn't entirely the case. The nonsense we talked of was less a focus and more of a barrier for my thoughts on last night's disaster.

What a fool I was to approach them! I was a stranger on their island with less right to stand on their temple grounds than my own colleagues. This might have been my one chance to learn something true and important on this blasted expedition. And I squandered it! I practically let my only lead walk away! Perhaps everyone at the journal was right in describing my character as lazy instead of cautious.

My distaste for the field of archaeology had somehow shifted to a hatred of my own inadequacies. I could never live up to what I expressed in my articles.

Suddenly, I felt a pat on my back and the most surprising thing about this journey so far occurred. Adrien Fischer was up early and ready to depart. He brought his cocky grin to the seat beside me and ordered a coffee from one of the waitresses, asking it to 'be hurried along' and 'to make it from her heart' in broken Greek which only achieved in making the woman look both of us over with disgust.

Adrien waved her reaction off before conversing with me. "Never had a chance to talk last night, Edward. Did you figure anything out from your stakeout?" He jested without any idea what had taken place last night at the site. I found his words amusing for a second, but that was shortly replaced with contempt when I realized who had spoken them.

"We aren't going to find anything out like this, Adrien." I spoke more into my espresso than to him.

"Hey, we're going to find something. We've still got a few good days left of digging to do before we set off for home. We'll find something. We have to."

I paused. The inflection of his voice was off. Almost dire. I didn't want to address it, but, thankfully, Fischer seemed bent on clearing it up for me. "I know of your situation, Edward. Not because most of the people at the journal have been talking about you behind your back. No. It's because, you see, my neck is also on the chopping block."

I turned to see a new desperation in his gaze. He smoldered with a cup of coffee now in his hands from the perturbed waitress. "I had one bad article, Edward. I was working a site around the Cape of South Africa. We dug for days looking through this ancient tribe's burial mound in hopes of finding something. It was on the last day. I found a mask. An actual mask! I was so thrilled and relieved that I didn't think much of the article. I just sent the find back home to Cassius Drake's estate."

Drake. The man was intolerable. No one could rival his disrespect for the study, and I had written a dozen articles on the importance of demolishing the practices of private collections in the past. Things started to click even before Fischer finished his tale and I rested my chin on my fist while watching ships pass through Mytilene's harbor.

"Well, when I came back. I wrote my article and sent it in. I thought everything was fine until the journal sent it back to me with a letter of refusal that threatened to prosecute me. Turns out, Drake had one of his guys who worked with me write up an article and twisted the narrative to show that he found the mask instead of me. Then, Drake forwarded the paper along and... well, my research was too late. They took my discovery from me. They said..."

He grew more emotional by the second. The wind was getting a little restless by the shore and I noticed the dockworkers struggle with keeping the boats at bay.

"I am going to be excommunicated from the field if I don't get this right, Edward! All because of Drake!" He slammed his fist into the table to get the point across and I was jarred out of my thoughts.

"What are you asking of me, Adrien?"

"You are brilliant, Edward. You know more about this study than I even do. So, I need you to focus. No more standing aside, afraid to get your hands dirty. I need you to find something. You can write the article. I don't care. All I ask is that you put my name on it as well. Please, I am begging you here."

The man was about ready to get on his hands and knees in case I didn't believe his desperation, but I nodded understandingly towards him. I had no intention of doing it, but I thought it might help ease his mind until he mistakenly found something in the dirt and no longer needed me. For that was the man, Adrien Fischer was. A leech.

"I'll get to work, Adrien. You should get the group together. We leave in ten minutes."

"Thank you, Edward. Thank you!"

With that, I started making my way back to the inn where I prepared myself for another useless day of desecrating what once was the most beautiful temple on Lesbos. The horses were a tad unruly this morning, likely because the cold weather was stiffening their joints. However, most of the morning and afternoon went by as one would expect. It wasn't until later in the day when I received an unlikely visitor.

Still seated beside the temple grounds, despite my promise to Adrien, I was welcomed by an unlikely companion. The old woman who I had seen leading the sect of followers in a prayer last night suddenly materialized by my side. Her tan skin was wrinkled with more than sixty years of life. She was wearing a beige blouse with a grey woolen sweater wrapped around her shoulders. For the first few minutes, neither of us said a word. We just sat there and watched the students dig up the Earth and comb through rubble with large brushes.

"There's nothing of value here," she said in a rough voice and with a throaty Greek accent.

I nodded in kind. "Perhaps not anything of monetary value. But I didn't come here for those same trinkets they dig for."

She slowly raised her hand over to the northern hill. "The Catholic church. Years ago, when men came to observe the temple, they found nothing. The church was here before your people. They already pillaged and toppled this temple over. Called it pagan and such."

Obviously, when the Holy Roman Empire spread their borders, they would have raped this land of jewels and sacred texts. Likely, the church was being built while their soldiers tore down the last remnants of Greek culture. Erasing…

"The altar? The church were the ones who scraped off the names. Why?"

Her face soured. "The third altar was built after the ones for Dionysus and Zeus. My ancestors restored it, maintained it after the men ransacked the temple. It is sacred to us."

"Of course," I tried to speak as much sympathy into my words as possible. "No one has any right to destroy what your people constructed. Especially not us. However, I am curious. Whose altar is it dedicated to anyway?"

"It was not rebuilt by us for any one Greek god or goddess. It… well, it is difficult to explain to someone like you."

I smiled. "Try me."

The woman looked around us to see if anyone was listening in on our conversation before leaning in closer to me. "I can't explain it. No one can. There… is a feeling we get when we are here. This place and its history. We don't worship the gods, but the delicate fire in our flesh."

She was right. It was confusing. What did she mean by each of us? The people of Lesbos or her sect of followers? And this feeling she was trying to describe. What history did this temple grounds hold that past excavations had yet to uncover? There were so many questions and I just looked upon her tired face with a dumbstruck expression plastered on my own. "I-I—I have so many questions. Who are you? Why do you sneak into the temple at night? Why was your altar created? What happened here that spurred all of this on? Please, you must tell me."

Her blank stare made me realize that I had pushed too hard for an explanation, and I cursed myself for rushing my own research. Her lips twisted upturned, as if she had sewn her own mouth shut. When I realized that she wouldn't tell me, I turned back around to face the slowly drooping sun with her at my side. We watched its descent together in utter silence.

A few minutes later, the woman stood up and was about to set out back to the dirt path when she hunched down over my shoulder. "Join us. Tonight." She spoke quickly, suddenly, yet not menacingly as I had anticipated after my intrusion. And then she was off.

I felt lost. Like nothing she had said to me made any sense and, instead of answering my important questions, only created new barriers between me and what I wanted to find out. I knew then that I must come back to the temple grounds tonight. I needed to get to the bottom of this before my time on Mytilene was cut short.

Soon, the day's efforts were complete, and our group headed back into town. Fischer had chosen to ride his horse alongside mine and we made short banter of what each of our teams had discovered in today's dig. There wasn't much besides some pottery shards, which Adrien saw as worthless and an insignificant find. I kept quiet most of the time to avoid starting any more arguments with the man. Oddly, his character had somehow changed around me. He was no longer this cocky adventurer with a million famed discoveries under his belt. No. Now, he was much more like the students we were meant to advise on our excavation. I feared that when we reached the inn, he would be following me at my coat tails.

It was an almost shocking transformation that only complicated my decision in not helping him with his research. After all, he wasn't posing to be the greatest in the field anymore. Now, he was furthermore pathetic and pitiable. I chose to delay my decision in helping Fischer since, at this moment in time, I, myself, did not have any research to report on and could not share any information on the third altar. Whether or not I would assist him in restoring his credibility, I chose to push off on another day when I actually had something of value to tell.

Soon we arrived back in town and Fischer, thankfully, took off with the rest of the students to grab dinner from a local eatery. Everyone seemed to be a bit moody today, including Beatrice who seemed on the verge of having a mental breakdown over Fischer's impractical procedures on the dig site.

Yet, she did seem to be keeping something back from our open conversation and I made a mental note of her hesitation. Had she found something? Had she learned what I had last night? About the sisterhood? There was no way to be certain since Beatrice didn't feel like sharing her knowledge with me just yet.

When we arrived back at the inn, Adrien put on that cheeky smile and grouped everyone together for another night of revelry in Lesbos. I chose to head back to my room and made up an excuse that I had notes to detail which might point us in new directions for our excavation. It wasn't a total lie, but I did not see the point in informing Adrien of my discovery until I possessed substantial evidence. He nodded and I got prepared for another night out at the temple grounds.

I was tired and almost regretting my choice to lose another night's rest. However, the opportunity to uncover the truth behind a nameless altar enticed me, rejuvenating my spirit with the potential of figuring out an impossibly ancient mystery. I waited until the sky darkened before hiking back out onto the dirt path. The temple grounds were a bit far from Mytilene, but the much-needed exercise helped keep my mind focused on the task at hand.

I contemplated the altar even more the closer I was to the dig site. The stone had been completely marred by the Catholic Church upon their arrival in the early years of the

Holy Roman Empire. The church was known for decimating any form of culture that opposed their own beliefs and the shared history with the Greeks meant nothing to Catholic rule. It was common practice to destroy another society's structures or art and then construct a 'purer' Catholic structure beside or on top of the ruins. Romans also liked to adopt what fit their interests and shun that which was foreign or heathen. For instance, the Romans targeted Hellenistic sculptures rather than Classical art pieces since Romans adored the more god-like Greek style instead of something more muted and realistic. This applied similarly in architecture, such as columns.

This particular temple was hard to date since Ionic columns have been known to the Greek world all the way back in the archaic period. Without any artifacts or statues remaining in the temple, it was difficult to discern the true date with the tools I had in hand. However, the lack of any Corinthian columns at this site suggested it to be older than the Hellenistic period. The more I thought of the Ionic ram-horned shape, the more I pictured the Temple of Athena in my head and the goddess' grace reassured my theories.

So, the church must have had another reason to destroy the temple. This brought my thoughts back to the third altar. They specifically targeted it, as seen in the scratch marks in the altar floor and rubble. Despite being kept intact by this sect of followers, there was no longer a trace of evidence that could lead back to the original design. The Romans were thorough in eradicating history, which has made my life as a historian quite frustrating. Though, the act itself was, alone, significant enough.

Therefore, with no more information on the site, my mind drifted to the crowd of robed figures from last night. They were the key to figuring out this puzzle. Their connection to the altar, it was sacred to them. Yet, perhaps it wasn't so much the altar that was sacred, so much as they were to each other. My reasonings for this were there decisions not to repair the altar. They maintained the foundations, but they never rebuilt. And if this deity were important to them, why wouldn't they construct a new altar in secret from the church.

The biggest connection between the worshippers is that they were all women. Their gender clearly played an important role in this nightly meeting. Not to mention, my mere presence seemed to disrupt their gathering. So, it was safe to assume that no man partook in these events.

Was this sect particular to Greece, or only to Lesbos? If Greece, then where was it started? And if Lesbos, then what connection did…

I paused on the dirt path, breathing in the night air like cigar smoke in my lungs. A chill, not from the cold weather, ran down the nape of my neck as I realized what I was chasing after. The words of the woman at the temple

came back to my ears in a hollow voice. *We don't worship
the gods, but the delicate fire in our flesh.*

Only then did it all start to click.

Chapter 10

The moon shone like a sparkling gem through a blanket of black sky hanging over a dry, cold forest of olive trees. The farmers had left late in the afternoon yet had neglected many of their tools. Most remained propped up against a low-hanging bough with no real value and therefore no threat to thievery. The path was silent save for some nightly critters singing their final tunes before drooping into a comfortable slumber. Not a soul moved. Then, from up the dirt road crafted by ancient hands and tools, dark cloth robes and shawls moved with the bobbing of heads. Voices whispered like the rubbing of dry leaves. Each approached the temple grounds with apprehension upon spotting my figure sitting beside one of the marble columns at the unnamed altar.

I spied the older woman near the rear of the group of women, taking her time with each careful step and calming some of the concerned followers who dropped back to question her motives. She smiled at me that wrinkly grin I was met with earlier in the day and I felt reassured in my answers. The followers started to gather around the altar in a semicircle, including me who remained seated until the brunette arrived. She glared at me with those ferocious green eyes, and I averted her gaze momentarily to steel myself. She approached me and I was forced to stand up. I had dreaded this moment for the past few hours as I was still ashamed of my actions from last night.

She went to speak, but the older woman stepped in before she could vocalize any threats. "Thank you for joining us," she paused.

"Edward," I reached out my hand.

"Myrine" she shook my hand, making a show of it for the others. "This is Ekaterina. She manages our meetings." The old woman introduced us calmly, despite the clear tension in the air.

"As well as decides who can join in…" Her voice was deeply pitched with words crisp in the fall air.

"I am honored to have been invited, Myrine."

She took some steps back to stand beside the altar while Ekaterina took her place at my side to keep an eye on my behavior, I suspect.

"The evening chill does not still the warm beating of our living hearts. Tonight's procession will hopefully explain to you our need for secrecy."

"And then you can take your friends and leave this island." Ekaterina whispered under her breath just loud enough for me to hear.

"Please, save your questions until after the ceremony, Edward. Then, my sisters and I will explain everything to you. Our cause and your being here tonight."

The words were weighty and the stares I received only filled the air with more strain than the previous night. Yet, I held strong and gave a nod of my consent. There were few questions left, except one, and I knew that it would be answered shortly.

Myrine waivered and then everyone bowed their heads, me following suit. Their words, at first, were a dissonant rumble that my ears could not decipher. A mumble that was out of tune with my own world. Then, I breathed in some of the night air, feeling the island carry my feet across Poseidon's domain. The northern winds pressed into me cold air that shook the trees around us. From their smallest branches to the roots birthed in Gaia's bones. I felt the world around me and breathed its essence in. Only then, did I hear their words.

"—the swift Sparrows that brought you black Earth—"

"—glittering minded, deathless one—"

"—nectar in golden cups—"

"—Lydian chariots—"

"Shivering with sweat, cold tremors—"

Myrine's words echoed the loudest. "My voice goes. My tongue freezes. Fire, delicate fire, in the flesh. Blind, stunned, the sound of thunder in my ears."

Confidently, I followed in stride with her words until I remained the only one speaking the rhymes. "I turn the color of dead grass, and I'm an inch from dying."

I didn't realize how reserved each of the followers had become until I finished the famous rhyme and Myrine's face blossomed with warmth in her cheeks. Even Ekaterina seemed surprise in my own knowledge of Mytilene's historic poetry. She was stunned with her mouth agape in the middle of another poem.

I took a step forward. "This altar, the deity, that isn't what brings you back here."

Myrine shook her head and I continued to elaborate.

"Sappho. The tenth muse of the ancient world. She was

born in Eresos, here on Lesbos, and her poetry, well, its

romantic descriptions of the female form were likely seen

as blasphemous by male-dominated communities and the

Catholic church. Enough that they would scrub any

inscriptions from temple walls and burn all scrolls and

poems detailing her tragic life."

I looked over at Myrine for confirmation and she nodded

for me to keep going, so I did. "You meet in secret.

Persecution still dominates Lesbos even centuries after the

rule of the Holy Roman Empire. You come here at night

because this was where Sappho celebrated her first

Thesmophoria Festival. This is where she read out her first

poem she wrote at Mytilene's schools for young women.

You come here to celebrate her legacy and to carry on

those traditions. An astonishing feat."

I paused. "I suppose, there is only one question I do have.

Why invite me back here? If this place is so sacred to your

group, why allow me, a man, anywhere near here after

what your people have been through? Especially after my intrusion last night?”

The women looked at me with the same confusion I was now wearing on my face, and it was Ekaterina, not Myrine, who answered the question on all of our minds. “Because your friends are looking to uncover our secret. If word gets out about our gatherings, they will exaggerate. They will demonize us, make us sound like witches. That’s not who we are. Some of us are looking to heal from ugly pasts.” Her voice waivered. “Some of us have been ostracized for the ones we love.”

“And some of us are here to support our sisters in need,” Myrine chimed in. “Just as Sappho did for our ancestors. My ancestors.”

I nodded, suddenly the message cleared up in my mind. “You want me to keep my team away from leaking your secrets to the world. Still, why? It seems to me that you aren't doing anything wrong. In fact, I feel like your sisterhood is quite admirable. Why not spread your ideals elsewhere to places where other women might be in need of your support? Why not let yourselves be known?"

Ekaterina fiercely returned. "Sadly, the world does not think like you, Edward. They would find our meetings secular and see it as something they can't have. We would be excommunicated from our own society and our meetings would cease to function without the prodding of man's world. As is the case for everything, if it doesn't align with your world then it should be destroyed." She stared me down, speaking pointedly.

Myrine took a stance beside me, still a little hunched in her gray shawl. "It's true, Edward. Just look at what your society have done to everything Sappho created. They won't accept us. You can't tell them anything."

I took a step back, suddenly panicked by the number of eyes on me and the great decision that they had presented me unexpectedly. I came here tonight to find out more of what was going on at this altar and discover the name of the deity it belonged to. Instead, I figured out that the women of Lesbos were not worshipping a god, so much as they were celebrating the courageous practices of the poet, Sappho. They came here, not out of worship, but for the love and support of their sisterhood. The mere concept of their caring group was impossible for me and my gender to fully grasp, but I was thankful that they allowed me to come here tonight.

To simply have a glimpse into their world, a longstanding ancient practice, was worth more than any gold scepter or pharaoh's tomb. Still, there was one thing nagging me at the base of my skull.

This was not something I could write in an article for the *Archaeologia*. Although an impressive find, I could not, in good conscience, reveal their existence to the world and sell them out for a spot at the journal. Although I didn't know any of these women, they had brought me here out of desperation as seen in their pleading and distrustful gazes. They wanted me to stop my expedition from uncovering their way of life. And yet, why me? I doubted my word could change that of Adrien Fischer if he found them out as easily as I had. I no longer had any sway at the journal. Did they simply bring me here because I knew their secret and therefore posed a threat? Then why even bring me back here and let me in on their practices for Sappho?

Perhaps chance was involved. I had a streak of bad luck and maybe the goddess Nike saw it fit to throw me a bone for my research article. Unlikely, but a good researcher should never doubt the probability of impossible odds. After all, that was what made up most of our findings today. Blind luck.

I realized that they were still waiting for me to say something, and I took a seat on one of the marble columns to collect my thoughts. I couldn't help but feel like they brought me here for a reason besides keeping a secret. Otherwise, they would have simply ignored me and waited for my team to leave the island. So, why did Myrine reach out to me and let me join in on tonight's procession?

They offered no hints toward their intentions and, thus, I would need to wait for more evidence to further explain their intentions. Biding my time seemed like the safest bet. I took in a deep breath before letting it flutter a warm cloud in the night air, seething from my lips.

"This is important. For all of you. Whatever wrongs my world has done to yours, I cannot condone or even begin to repay. You've brought me here on good faith that I will keep your secret. I am grateful of being privy to your world. I will not speak a word to my team and will dissuade their efforts in uncovering your doings at this third altar.

The only thing I must ask is the opportunity to better understand your muse, Sappho."

The temple was eerie with each cloaked figure glancing at one another with nervous expressions, waiting for their group to decide whether or not to accept my bold terms. Perhaps it was cold of me to proposition them with a counteroffer, but I could not give up the chance to learn more about a historical figure who has been long dead and whose history was nearly eradicated from the records. Also, this was my one chance of discovering something worthy of keeping my position on the journal since the temple grounds were barren.

"Her works, although now only fragments, were some of the most beautiful verses ever spoken in the ancient world. To hear those words once again spoken at this temple centuries later, it's been quite the blessing. Since her history is so closely tied to your own," I directed towards Myrine, "I believe it is safe to say that you know more about her character than any living being. I would very much love to hear you recount these stories to me.”

Ekaterina posed defensively besides Myrine. Some of the crowd shifted with the same worried look on their faces. “Why? What interest do you have in our sister?”

I paused. “I’ve come here with no intentions of defaming her character more than the Catholic church already has done. If that’s why you think I came back here tonight, then you’ve gotten me all wrong. I—I have a passion for history, and not in the kind I read in books, but the kind I see and hear for myself. This opportunity… I would be ever grateful to hear your ancestors’ side of history.”

Ekaterina seemed ready to pounce, but Myrine held out her wearied arm and stopped her. “My ancestors’ side of the story is one buried by man’s world. It is the story of Sappho’s lover.”

My heart stopped. “The ferryman?”

She grinned. "The Ferry woman."

Chapter 11

Soon after our long discussion at the temple grounds, the sisterhood of Sappho and I reached an agreement where I would not discuss their practices as well as impede the meddling of my troupe of archaeologists so long as I could visit Myrine's home each night and listen to her stories. It was quite a shocking turn of events and, after my hike back to the town of Mytilene, I was completely drained of all physical effort. I faintly recall walking into my room and dropping atop my mattress before passing out due to exhaustion. My dreams were of a past world. Men and women carrying jars of honey and dragging carts filled with the freshest smelling bread. Fields of flowers bowed to the weight of the eastern winds and children chased each other with twigs they snapped off of young olive trees. Their concerns were of physical welfare. Food from their wood ovens, water from their fresh springs, and a warm shelter with few holes where they could rest their heads at night. They lived. Not for fame or wealth like the stories they told one another. They lived freely.

My dreams were dashed by a knocking on my door, and I regretted sleeping in late another day. I made quick to answer the call and was surprised to find two guests bickering at my doorstep. Their voices were far too hushed for me to understand, and they silenced as soon I pulled open the door. Adrien Fischer arrived with the most forced welcoming expression on his face and two cups of coffee in his hands. Beside him, glaring at the fool, Beatrice had a handful of papers under her arms.

"Edwa—"

"Davenport!" Fischer abruptly rushed in ahead of Beatrice's greeting and then, physically, pushed his way into my room.

I looked over at him, slightly perturbed, while he set up our mugs of coffee at my small breakfast table by the window overlooking Mytilene. Beatrice was equally annoyed at Fischer's presence, hefting up her papers before they fell out from under her arms. A small sheet broke free and I picked it up off the ground and handed it to her. I only got a second to look it over and my face paled.

The words "third altar" and "Sappho" were both present in the writing and I feared that my promise to the women of Lesbos might prove difficult to keep after all. Beatrice didn't appear to notice my dour look, likely putting it to waking with Fischer at my doorstep.

"Another time then, I assume," her smile drew inward, disappointed.

I nodded. "We'll talk about, whatever it is, later. Right now, I need to deal with this braggart."

"I do not envy you."

She turned on her heel and headed down the corridor, still shuffling with the papers in her arms. I spied after her, my thoughts lingering on what she might have been researching in regard to the third altar. Was she aware of the women who worshipped there at night? Could she have spied on them as I had?

A pat on my shoulder gave me a slight fright, jumping up in my day-old clothes that were still covered in dirt and grime. I felt a bit of a mess, but Fischer didn't seem to care. He practically dragged me over to the table so that we might have our coffee together. Something was a tad off about him today. He was all excited over something, likely nothing, but I was so peeved by his forced enthusiasm that even my coffee couldn't improve my mood.

"Good morning, Edward! It is another day, another chance to find our saving grace! I'll be honest, I have an excellent feeling that today will be the day."

"Perhaps," I nodded.

"Oh, don't be so down. It's not over until it's over and Adrien Fischer won't leave until we've found the next tomb of Alexander the Great!" Hearing him use his own name just about incited in me a bout of nausea.

"No one has even found the actual tomb of Alexander the Great," I corrected him, but he glossed over my comment with speed.

"I can tell that we will find something. You know why? Because we just aren't the type of researchers who get thrown out. Not us. Why, I once knew a guy, Terrence Gessler. Tampered with his research and was found out by his expedition team. The guy wouldn't stop clamoring that what he found was legitimate. He brought it up with the journal and they took his credentials away from him. Word is that he still claims this tablet or whatever he found was truly an original artifact."

"And was it?"

"Of course not! Gessler got it from an antique shop in

Berlin and planted it at the site."

Fischer leaned in uncomfortably close to me. "That's how I

know we aren't going to lose out on our titles, Eddie.

Despite everything we've done, we are still honest with one

another. What we find, we'll use to help each other.

Right?"

Wrong. If a man like you, Fischer, discovered the followers

of Sappho, then you would sell each of them out in a

heartbeat. You'd write their names up and down your

article and still denounce each of their stories in favor of

what the church has been peddling out for centuries.

And yet, I pondered his choices as if they were my own.

Was I not trying to do the same thing? Using their history,

their treasured past to protect my own name from the

journal. How could I write an article on their celebrated

poetess without bringing up how I learned of their ancestral tales?

Then again, how could I not? Like Archie said, I had a right to take care of my own interests. Why shouldn't I preserve my name? After all, how could I change the world of archaeology if I lost my credibility?

Still, the cost taxed me and my reasonings which only now sounded remarkably similar to Fischer's own.

Finally, I broke my silence. "Right. We are much unlike Gessler."

We spoke of the dig site and the lack of finds we've made so far. Fischer's optimism was almost toxic to my aching ears, and I felt a headache once again forming on this trip. We finished our coffees and he hurried off to ready our horses and the students for another workday. I felt terribly conflicted and remained in my room watching the ebb and flow of the Aegean rock the ships docked down below.

Men and women scurried through the streets and the warmth unfamiliar to the fall air helped calm my uneasy mind. I felt an incredible urge to walk the streets once more. Decidedly so, I set out to explore some more of the local shoppes and site. Flower shops, bakeries, antique stores with funny little dolls. I even ran into Jayson on his way up to the olive forests. He waved me over and we chatted about the pleasant weather before he hopped on a wagon with four other men whom I recognized from his group. His smile never faded even after the wagon was too far along the trail for me to see, but I simply knew it remained.

I kept roaming the streets until Oliver came up to me, out of breath, and informed me in a pert manner that the crew would be leaving soon and that I needed to hurry if I wanted to hear Fischer's speech. Supposedly, he had written something on paper to cheer the spirits of the students and would be reading it along their travels to the temple grounds. Already satisfied with my current migraine, I sent Oliver back along his way and informed him that I would catch up to the team later in the afternoon. He was only a bit disappointed in my decision, but quickly ran back up the hill in hopes of making it in time for Fischer's speech himself.

I spent a few moments walking around this Roman fountain that was in need of repair. The once powerful geyser that sprung free from the Earth was now nothing more than a dribble, echoes of a long dead empire. Even after learning what the Romans had done to the women of Mytilene, my curious eyes still marveled at their architecture which remained standing even under the control of the Ottomans.

The construction alone was worth studying and I was curious why the remains of a desecrated temple proved more significant in the eyes of my colleagues instead of the structures that surrounded us. Why disturb the dead and the victims of persecution? Why, when we could learn more about the Greco-Roman occupation of this island right here! We turn over loose stones, destroying whatever remained of their ruins when there are buildings from centuries ago which stand amongst the present city.

Perhaps I was simply trying to find a way to avoid the inevitable confrontation over Myrine's secret. I had prayed that none other than myself would figure out their truth and that this trip would be a simple dig where we all go home empty handed. Yet, Beatrice figuring out Sappho's connection to the site would only push her on the same track I was mere days ago. If I approached her and dissuaded her from pursuing—

No. I could not do that. Not to Beatrice. She was not only a respectable colleague, but also someone I'd call a friend. No. I'd need to figure out what other options were available to me before resorting to something so cold.

I started back to the inn and saddled up on the lonely lame mare that was left for me. I thought hard on how to approach Beatrice while hiking up the trail. Not much came to the forefront of my mind. Mostly maybes, and nothing I truly felt comfortable with saying in order to ruin her efforts.

All of it vacated my mind once I approached the dig site. Remarkably, it wasn't completely decimated by the time I got there. Of course, that wasn't saying much. Many of the stones which created the path to the temple foundation were now tossed aside in favor of new grids which the students laboriously dug up. It was an absolute massacre.

Thankfully, none of my own designated groups had ripped up the Earth around the third altar just yet. Their spades and trowels were at the ready, but I motioned for them to stand down and set them up with a new task. They each frowned, replacing their weapons of destruction aside in favor of brushes to help preserve the pristine altar rock. The students pouted, calling me names behind my back, and I let them. Perhaps their consciences would thank me in a few years.

The day went by slowly and I prayed that Beatrice would wait until tonight to approach me with her theories. Alas, I was not that lucky.

Her button-up was tarnished by the dirt and mud from digging out the site floor and her hair, tussled like a rat's nest. Beatrice approached me with a smile, but I knew from its wavering expression that she was at her wits end as to what to do with Fischer's blatant disrespect for ethical procedures. She had the papers back under her arm and motioned for me to follow her to a more private spot for our conversation. I obliged and we took seats on tree stumps out in the olive forest. My eyes were more focused on the apple tree we were sitting beneath than the plans she spread out on a small boulder in between us. Was the apple tree here before the olive farm or did they plant it here after? It appeared out of place, and I shared the same sentiment as of right this moment.

"Look, I've done some research at the local library. I wanted to learn more about the island since nothing Fischer has ordered us to do has come up with anything of value."

"And? What did you find out?" I pretended to not be interested, which wasn't one of my strong suits.

"Well, not much. The only thing any book has recorded pertaining to this site is what the last team of archaeologists which visited here stated nearly two decades ago. But I got to asking some of the townsfolk after your little argument with Fischer over the third altar."

Oh, no. What if she approached one of the followers? What if they believed I had leaked my discovery with Beatrice? Then, all of my efforts to learn more about Sappho would be for naught!

"The altar. I believe it belongs to a goddess. Cybele to be precise. She's more known to be worshipped in Anatolia, not Greece. There's a long history at this temple with women—"

"Yes, of course. But why do you believe it's Cybele?" I tried to change the subject.

She smirked. "I thought about the island. Our proximity to the Asia Minor and the supposed location of the ancient Minoan civilization, if we are to believe Arthur Evans' research, then that would suggest a belief in the Phrygian mother goddess. Plus, the roundness of the stones at the third altar suggest to me that the statues there were larger than that of Zeus and Dionysus. No other Greek goddess, not even Hera, would need that much space for display."

Curious. Why hadn't I thought of that? The stone foundation was particularly more circular at my altar than the other two, but I had simply chalked that up to the weathering away of rock. Foolish, I'd need to correct my notes when I returned to my room later tonight.

"Interesting. I think you have a solid theory here, Beatrice."

"That's not all," her real smile with the crooked teeth returned. "The presence of the mother goddess is more indicative of the site at large. Think about it. This was where the ancient Greeks of Mytilene held their town meetings and community events! The celebration of this goddess there, and what I've learned from the locals, suggests female leadership on Lesbos. The local people I talked with described ceremonies similar to pageant shows and, most importantly, poetry readings."

My heart dropped. My bones felt hollow in my body, and I just about fainted on the spot.

"One woman in particular was famous for her performances at this site—"

"Sappho." I answered before she had time to finish.

She cocked her head. "That's right. How did you know that?"

I shook my head and got up from my seat to leave. "Beatrice, we will have to discuss this later. The sun is setting, and I have my own research I must conduct before we all head back into town."

"You didn't answer my question," she sounded a tad annoyed whilst rustling up her documents from the rockface.

I paused in the forest and spied a few young apples sitting in the tree's bough. They weren't ready for harvest yet, but they soon would carry patches of red.

"I'm afraid that we've run out of time today. You know that we can't leave Fischer too long alone or else he might try and carry each of the marble columns back to London on his shoulders." I smiled back at her to ease her confusion.

Hardly, but Beatrice seemed content enough to wait for my response and I was thankful for the time. I quickly rushed off through the forest, happy to see the temple grounds weren't eradicated by incompetency just yet and rode my lame mare up the dirt path to where I suspected Myrine's hut resided in hiding.

Chapter 12

Myrine's home was only a kilometer or so up the rolling hill where the forests started to give way to a bald hillock. Wild grasses and flowers flourished unchecked by the natives and there was a sense of calm achieved by the setting sun which cascaded a burnt orange across the landscape. Huts of rock and brick were scattered across the hilltop, each slightly more lopsided than the other. As I progressed north through their little community, I felt the weight of stares on my shoulders. Through the windows, I knew that the women, owners of the homes, were watching me pass through their sanctuary. It was too early for the men to come home from harvesting the forests or working the docks and the presence of a foreigner likely unsettled them. If I was any other man from my troupe of expeditioners, then I would likely have been sent back down the hill. Yet, my journey north was never pestered.

As the hill began to slope back down into the heart of Lesbos' island, their remained a tiny home made up of rocks ranging in sizes. There was something primordial of its structure. Perhaps it was the lack of the brick shingles reminiscent of the Romans or the decorative lotus windows inherited by the Ottomans. You could just picture ancient hands dragging rock and wood up the hillside, spending a few weeks preparing a new home for their family.

I could tell that this hut belonged to Myrine.

I approached the door cautiously and rapped a few knocks on the door. The latch was unlocked, and the door pulled open, but not by the short, hunched Myrine, but by Ekaterina. She coldly glared at me, obviously still upset with me and my intrusion the other night. I gave her a polite nod. "Greetings! It is shaping up to be a beautiful night, isn't it?"

She stayed her glare on me for a second before stepping aside to let me enter the hut. Her silence was threatening enough to make me reconsider meeting with Myrine, but I had come too far now to stray from my course.

The inside of the hut was little better than the outside. The floors were wooden, except for the kitchen which was marble, and the walls were cleverly decorated with the kind of paintings I saw in the antique shop down in Mytilene. Yet, the illustrations were less crisp. The paint seemed closely tied to the canvas in a way that made me question the authenticity of the ones I saw in the store. This building was unlike any other I had seen on this island. There was a sense of life, like somehow you knew that it was a home and not a ruin.

Myrine was seated in a wooden chair beside a small fireplace. She was stoking the flames with a dull-looking rod of steel and her eyes were emblazoned by the bright light as I approached to take a seat next to her. She smiled wryly at me. "Evening, Edward. Ekaterina believed you wouldn't show."

I gave the woman to my left a sly wrinkle of a grin. "Yes, well, we didn't necessarily get off on the right foot. Unlike my colleagues, my passion stems not from material wealth or getting my name chiseled on plaques."

"That remains to be seen," Ekaterina whispered loud enough for me to hear before heading back out of the hut.

I waited for the door to shut behind her before conversing with the old woman, Myrine. I leaned forward in my seat. "Before we get started, there is something that I must make you aware of. I—I would like to learn of Sappho's history because I'd like to chronicle it. Write down what truly happened instead of what soldiers and priests have muddled. Of course, I understand if you think that is breaching our agreement since I stated I would not share your existence with the world, but—"

"You want to tell her story?" she said in an all-knowing manner that the wise and elderly each possessed.

I nodded. "I won't tell a soul about your sisterhood. I find what you do something modern society could learn from, but that isn't my secret to share. However, I do believe that Sappho's story has been robbed from her and her ancestors. That is why I want to write it down."

She paused, then nodded. "I have no issues with that. Nor do I believe my sisters will, besides Ekaterina. She is… apprehensive towards this whole ordeal."

"I can tell."

"Don't misjudge her," Myrine warned me, the tone in her voice growing more serious by the second. "Ekaterina tried to do what you wanted us to do. To tell the world. She spoke to the last archaeologists. Her and her partner, Safia, tried to explain our story and our beliefs to them."

"Safia?" I questioned.

She smirked. "Don't sound surprised, Edward."

I wasn't, but the beliefs felt conditioned into my own diction from an early age. I apologized and Myrine carried on. "Safia was exiled. They put everything on her. That she was trying to defile the integrity of this island and rob men of their wives. Her whole life was ruined."

"Christ…"

"The church helped. They practically shunned her out of Mytilene and Safia was forced on the next boat off the island. Word got back that she grew ill on the trip and never made it to Corsica. The doctors called it one thing, but the women of the island know that it was heartbreak that took her life. Ekaterina hasn't been the same since. She was the one who spurred on Safia's ideas, and she feels partially at fault for the whole situation."

I was stunned. "I-I didn't realize."

Myrine grew quiet. "A terrible thing to lose. Love." Her voice grew distant as she recited rhymes into the fireplace. "Some say horseman, Some say warriors, some say a fleet of ships is the loveliest vision in this dark world. But I say it's what you love."

I remained silent until she finished the poem which I only recalled bits and pieces of from my time at university. When she was done with the lyrics, her mind returned to her home and her eyes entertained my presence. "There is only so much I can say. Much of what happened has been lost in the retelling of stories across generations."

I pulled out my notepad and pencil with an eagerness I hadn't felt in quite some time. "All the same, I'd love to hear what you have to say."

She smiled. "Okay then."

Hours went by. We started discussing Sappho's childhood on the forested island of Lesbos. She was born in Eresos to two wealthy political figures who controlled much of what happened on the island. She had three older brothers. Charaxus, Larichus, and Erigyius. They shaped up to be much like their father. Each had the gift of gab to fool an entire village that they were vital to the people's success, and they had no issue with abusing the hearts of young women. It was even believed that Charaxus ransomed off a young Egyptian girl to another elite politician for a wealthy sum.

Although Sappho also possessed the same attributed charisma as her brothers, her beliefs were strikingly ethical in comparison. Her mother died at a young age, but the last choice she made was to send her daughter off to a school whose goal was to busy the lives of young women in Mytliene.

"There she learned how to read and write poetry, I assume?" I quickly worked on my notes and asked for Myrine to slow down to give me time to my own thoughts.

She nodded, letting out a short laugh. "She practically taught them how to write it. She was a true natural, as my ancestors tell me. After all, she taught my—"

Her words jumbled together in my mind, struggling to translate Greek and write down my notes in English at the same time.

"Sorry, who did she teach."

"My ancestral mother." She spoke plainly, but the words didn't quite add up in translation.

"She taught your ancestors?"

"In a manner of speaking. She taught Cleis, who taught Zanya, who taught—"

"Cleis?" I was overwhelmed. The name was one I had learned of during my study of the island and of Sappho. However, the woman was still mystery to the whole study and to hear that she had a line of living descendants left me awestruck.

"Yes. My ancestral mother."

"Cleis? As in, Sappho's mother?"

"Sappho's mother was Cassandra, not Cleis. Cleis was her lover."

Suddenly, the room started to spin, and I stopped writing to see if Myrine was lying to me. Her face held its stern composure. She believed what she was telling me was the truth. A truth that I, only having heard it, was forced to question everything I knew of Sappho. Everything that I have ever read on her character. Everything the world has been told.

And those truths were always the most difficult ones to sell to any journal. As my mind began to question, my heart was slowly deflating.

For years, the community has been trying to track down Sappho's lineage through the scraps of tablets and poems which we have uncovered in the historical records written down by early historiographers in Athens. Sappho was a total mystery since all we possessed were bits and pieces and the occasional name. Cleis was a name many suspected to be the young mother of Sappho. However, now that might not be the case.

"Cleis. She went to the same school as Sappho?"

Myrine nodded. "That's where they met. That's where they learned poetry and, more importantly, their love for one another."

"Love? What about Kerkylas? Of Andros?" The name was one I had read about many years ago back in university and who many historians still believe to be Sappho's male lover.

This seemed to upset Myrine. Her face became embittered, and I worried that I was on the verge of being thrown out of her home. She breathed a deep sigh. "There was no Kerkylas. Are you aware of the name's translation?"

"I am."

"Then, you mustn't be foolish enough to believe what the church has told everyone about Sappho. There was no 'Dick' of Andros whom she married, as is Catholic tradition. That was all made up to subjugate Sappho's character to meet the expectations of your world."

Man's world. She didn't need to say it. I knew what she was harping on.

"And Cleis? Your ancestor? She was Sappho's lover then?"

Myrine nodded.

My mind was reeling at all the information I was learning in such a short time, more than what I had picked up at the Sanctuary of the Three Gods. If what Myrine was saying proved to be true, then it could completely change the way we see the poetess and her lyrical poetry forever. However, this all came with a big 'if' that I wasn't ready to believe. Still, I pushed my conscious doubt aside a little longer.

"So, they met at the school. Then what?"

"Well, that's when Sappho's career as the 'tenth muse' began at our temple. She read out her delicate pheromonal words to reach the ears of young woman's grasping heartstrings. And she did it all with Cleis. She was Sappho's inspiration. Their love brought a more emotional heat to the words which was unlike any other in the classical world. But… things soured when—"

"—the people found out about them."

She nodded. "The men came. They forced Sappho into exile. She was shipped off to Sicily like packaged goods!" Myrine's voice raised. "The damned fools! Ten years apart. They spent ten years away from one another's arms. Can you imagine? What that kind of torture could do to one's heart?"

She looked at me pleadingly.

My mind searched back through the years, but my heart had never yearned for another. Not as Sappho's had. So, I shook my head. "I cannot."

She returned her gaze to the fireplace and stretched out her hands to feel the warmth almost reassuring her that the fire was indeed real. "Cleis was devastated. She did not know what to do except wait for Sappho's return. During that time, she often met with the other women of Lesbos. That's where it all started. They supported Cleis in her difficult time, reassuring her that Sappho would one day return."

"And she did return." My mind tried to recount what I remembered of Sappho's history, before pausing at a rather hazy realization. "She returned. Spent her time spinning stunning lyrics for the people of Lesbos and reigniting her love for Cleis. She grew old. Her poems became famous all across Greece despite her being a woman poet. And…

And…"

Myrine's eyes fostered a glint of light from the fire, expressing a witty smile on her face. I looked closely trying to get a read whether or not the stories were true. Whether past historians had gotten Sappho's twilight years wrong like they had with Cleis. She noticed my apprehension and chose to break the silence for me. "Ask your questions, Edward."

The words wouldn't escape my lips, trapped in my throat for all lack of courage. So much I knew about Sappho was wrong. So much the world now knew was wrong! But her most tragic moment, her death, how could that be false? How could anyone lie about such a fateful ending? Still, my nerves kept my tongue in check. I averted my gaze in hopes of levying Myrine's weighted stare. My migraine returned achingly at the back of my skull.

"Ask," Myrine repeated.

Finally, my voice breached the noiseless hut. "I-Is… Is it true? When Sappho died… Her suicide at the Leucadian Cliffs? D-did her story end there?"

Time in the small Grecian hut slowed to a snail's pace. I felt my fingernails digging into the palm of my hand, waiting at shortened breaths for an answer. Myrine smiled, stoking the flames with her iron poker.

Then, she spoke. "No. None of it is true."

Suddenly, the chair was ripped out from underneath me. The feeling of falling, so closely tied with flying, struck me with total fear. For if one history could be fabricated, who was to say what we now know really did happen? Everything I had read, all that I had heard from lethargic professors at university came into question. How could I be certain any of it was true? I forgot how to breathe.

Instantly, I wanted to ask what actually happened to Sappho. How had her life ended? What became of Cleis?

How had the sisterhood survived for so long in hiding? But I stopped myself. Each question suddenly felt tart in my own mind. For I realized that none of it could possibly be proven true. Everything that Myrine had said up to this point was purely speculation without any actual evidence. There were no letters between the two lovers I could show to the journal. No fragmentary poems which described their relationship in detail. There was nothing to substantiate that any of the story had happened in the way she retold it.

All just here-say from an old woman and I cursed myself for being as fooled as I had to come here with the belief that I'd made the discovery of a lifetime.

I stood up from my seat to Myrine's shock and pocketed my notepad and pencil. I told her farewell in between her frustrated questions as to my behavior. Before I left the hut, I told her that I would come back tomorrow and that we would discuss the truth of the matter then. My gait was hurried down the hill and I felt those same nagging eyes on my back, which I politely ignored this time.

Chapter 13

As I was returning from Myrine's home, I decided to take a short detour into the woods in hopes of calming my mind enough to get my thoughts in order. The small stones by the apple tree from my last chat with Beatrice seemed like a good enough place as any to take a seat. So, I made my way back there and lowered myself onto a boulder of stone, shuffling my hands together in order to breathe some warmth into them on this frigid night.

Two rabbits crossed the forest floor ahead of my gaze which settled upon a rising crescent moon. My days on this island were numbered and I wasn't certain whether I was anxious because I would be leaving such a lovely place like Mytilene behind or because I would be coming home emptyhanded once more. I watched the little critters prance underneath the forest's overgrowth and imagined Sappho and Cleis doing the same many years ago.

A scowl spread across my face. I discarded the thought

from my mind and rested my head in my hands. Good God,

how could I have been so careless? To have fallen into such

a simple trap as is believing the lies of the old and

delusional. Edward, you came here preaching a code of

ethical and rational practices for the study of archaeology

and now you were doing the same thing as your colleagues.

How could you return to the journal and tell them such a

fantastical story with absolutely zero evidence or proof

from your dig site? Sure, she was a native. However, how

truthful could she be about something that happened

centuries ago?

I remembered each and every article I had submitted in the

past where I demonized the unlawful practices of other

archaeologists for lacking the proper skill in preserving

history. Now, here I sat upon a short rock thinking about

how I was about to do the exact same thing they did in

reporting a claim, throwing it out into the void of criticism, with nothing substantial behind itself.

"Fool," I mumbled to myself.

And if she were telling the truth?

"If? Ifs have no place in archaeology past the boundaries of theories, and theories didn't make glowing enough papers. The facts did." I reamed myself for even letting that tidbit of hope enter my mind once more.

I then thought of the journal and the impossible weight of their deadline plummeted my heart deep into the confines of my own stomach. The one thing I had feared might happen was beginning to play out before my very eyes. I was stuck at a site with no clear discovery in view. We were set to leave the island in less than two days' time. And I was in position to posit a spineless claim that my colleagues would rip to shreds as I had theirs. My head dropped further into my chest. Unlike before, there was no comforting hand to point me in the right direction like Archie had back at home.

The night drooped a dark blanket across my shoulders and the fatigue of the past few days started to wear me down. I felt like giving myself up to the elements right then and there. My limbs were shocked with pins and needles. I could just make out the presence of a single pearl gleaming up at me in the moonlight at the base of my rock. Part of me was curious as to what I had discovered, and I slowly leaned in a few inches to get a better look at what was stationed by me feet.

Then, the fear of being watched froze my bones solid in their body. It wasn't a single pearl, but two. Two large pearl eyes. Staring up at me with flashing teeth.

Its scaly body wriggled in the fallen tree leaves, crunching up the softness under the weight of its slimy body. I realized that I had locked eyes with a snake. More specifically, a Montivipera xanthina. Or as it was better known, an Ottoman viper.

It was approximately, sixty-five centimeters in length with dark black spots on its back and green camouflaged scales on the side which made it nearly impossible to discern its true size. Not only were its fangs venomous, but they weren't afraid of humans. They were an aggressive species.

We stared into one another's eyes, testing each other, looking for some kind of fault to use. Sweat formed on my brow despite the temperature being quite cool tonight. I wanted to shake, to scream even, but I knew that this would only aggravate the snake still seated at my feet.

Then, the strangest thing happened. Instead of thinking about how painful it would be to perish alone in these woods to the bite of an Ottoman viper, as many might, instead I thought only of Sappho.

I thought of her story, or the one that Myrine had described to me. I thought of how alone she must have felt in a family of men who had no issue with using women and abusing their emotions to gain political power. I thought of how frightening it must have been for her when she arrived at her school and locked eyes with Cleis for the first time and her heart skipped a beat. Was she as afraid of her feelings as I was of this viper right now? More so?

I thought of her exile. How could her friends and family react so harshly upon finding out that their young Sappho was in love with another, another who truly loved her?

I imagined her return, their embrace, the poetry that they must have created for one another. The beautiful feelings they shared that I could only, simply, begrudgingly, imagine now with death staring me down.

Death. Whether her suicide was factual or false, did that even matter? Myrine seemed less concerned with it than I had back at the hut. And was it so difficult for me to believe that the church had censored her story, having her love a man whose name translated to the male genitalia and jumping off the cliffs for the love of the ferryman? A loathsome stain on the truth!

Suddenly, I hated how history had abused her story. I hated everything which we now had to struggle to understand after most of what actually happened had been erased by men in power.

At that moment, I had my own venom.

And the Ottoman viper slithered away, back into the forest in hunt for another prey.

When it was out of eyesight, I realized how important this story was. Not for me, but for the sisters of Lesbos. They needed the truth out there. With my doubts subdued, I stood up from my seat and started to make my way back to

Mytilene with new purpose fueling the bitterness in my veins.

I was perhaps a few steps into the town center when I heard a shout call out my name in a slurred manner. It was Adrien Fischer. He was inebriated, likely after partaking in too much ouzo from the local tavern.

"Edward!" His shout was a mix of friendliness and loathing.

"Fischer," I tipped my head slightly to acknowledge his presence and hoped that was enough for tonight.

Still, he proceeded to follow me. "Edward! We need to talk!"

I was maybe six steps from the front door of the inn when Fischer reached me and clawed at my shoulder to face him. His breath reeked of alcohol and his clothes were stained with something equally foul-smelling. With droopy eyes and a bit of spittle on his lips, he pulled me around to confront him, something I was less inclined to do on an already hectic night.

"Edward!" he raised a pointed finger and jabbed it in my chest. "Tell me you've found something. Anything."

I brushed his hand aside. "Thought I did, but it turned out to be nothing," I lied.

He continued to eye me down through his heavy eyelids. "Edward, don't screw with me now! Tell me that you've dug something up! Tell me!"

His voice heated up, turning into angry shouts which bounced off the nearby stone buildings and pestered those asleep and the sleepless alike. I simply shook my head. "I've got nothing, Fischer."

This triggered him even more. He reached out with both of his bony hands and seized me by my shirt to grip me even closer to his odorous self. "Do you know what this means? What any of this means? We have two days! Two days to come up with something or our names are in ruins, and we start living like these poor bastards on this island! Two days! We've had about a week to dig something up and nothing! God, we are finished, aren't we?"

I struggled to push him free from me. "Get a hold of yourself!"

Adrien took a short tumble after I pushed him away, dropping to his knees. He breathed heavily, choosing to stay down instead of coming back up on his feet. "This is all your damn fault…" he whispered.

"Excuse me," I had just about had it with this man.

"I said, it's your damn fault!" He shouted up at me. "Every single day, you were sitting in the dirt doing nothing. I did all I could, pushed my team to dig further in hopes of finding something. Anything! And what did you do? You either leave early or refuse to partake in the dig site entirely! And what for? Are you expecting me to find something to save your name? Or…"

Fischer attempted to steady himself, rising back up to meet me. "Or what?" I asked.

He twisted his gaze aside, attempting to rediscover the thought that had escaped his drunken mind seconds ago. Then, a realization hit, and he peered up at me with a menacing snarl, like he was ready to rip at my throat.

"Or maybe you did find something and are keeping it to yourself?"

I stayed silent and I believed that was enough of an answer for him. He scoffed at me and turned on his heel.

"There is nothing worse in this life than a hypocrite."

Then, he was headed back to the tavern.

After being assaulted by Adrien Fischer, I finally made it to the safety of our inn and quietly climbed the staircase to reach my room. I was almost through the door when I heard the clearing of someone's throat break the silence of the inn's corridor. I felt robbed of my night's sleep that was mere feet away from me.

With my back turned, the voice spoke sharply. "You better make quick with the explanations, Edward."

It was Beatrice. Her arms were folded across her chest and her hair was tied up with a short black ribbon. She didn't have the papers from earlier in her possession at this moment, but I knew that this would likely be the bulk of our conversation.

I bowed my head and jutted a thumb towards my room. "Can this wait until the morning? I promise that I will explain everything to you then."

Perhaps my fatigue was just plain to see or maybe Beatrice was also beat from a long day at the temple grounds. Either way, she nodded her head.

"Tomorrow morning." She spoke sternly. "Promise?"

"I promise."

She turned around and headed back to her own room. As she left, an idea started to form in the back of my mind. It wasn't a plan just yet, but I believed that I could use Beatrice's curiosity to answer my own questions. A yawn reminded me of my body's lack of energy. I can't say that I remember much beyond falling into my bed with grimy clothes and Sappho's story still playing out in my dreams.

Chapter 14

I didn't stay asleep for very long, as my body had begged of me. Instead, I was bright eyed and dressed in a grey Saharan shirt and some old, roughed-up jeans that I found in my luggage. I took the time to clean myself up, shaving the stubble that had grown across my chin, combing my hair, and brushing my teeth. When I finished, I felt almost rejuvenated, save for the bags under my eyes. Those were inherent on an expedition such as this one.

The sun had just risen over the Aegean, and I left the inn to meet my olive farmer friends at the café. Jayson had just arrived with his pals, and I joined them in ordering a coffee with a single shot of espresso to prepare me for my day. It seemed that my worry was painted across my fatigued face since Jayson abruptly asked me what was troubling my conscience.

There was something almost thoughtful in the way Jayson spoke this morning that was dissimilar to each conversation we had previously entertained at this café. Usually, we would discuss meaningless things like the weather and each other's hometowns. Today, however; Jayson seemed more interested in myself than idle chatter.

"How much is truth valued?" I asked blindly.

It felt like a question that would fly over the poor olive farmer's head, but he instantly met my inquiry with a rebuttal.

"Depends. How many lies can you bear to tell?"

I was taken aback by his response. "And what if the lies are not our own?"

He sipped his coffee quietly to himself and took a few seconds to ponder. "Then the truth isn't either. Therefore, it has no value to anyone except for the owner."

My chest expanded with a heavy sigh, and I drank the bulk of my coffee before departing my group of friends. It was the first time in which I had left them seated at the cafe, and they all waved to me goodbye as I set off into the heart of Mytilene. I stopped at the bakery to meet with the workers and purchase some peinirli for Beatrice and myself.

As I was returning to the inn, I decided to make a stop at the antique shoppe. The vases were all replicas of ancient Greek pottery with a few nuances in the heroic paintings on their faces. A few Turkish copper rings caught my eye and the store owner tried hard to sell me on their exorbitant price. Lastly, I looked over a few of the Grecian dolls and figurines they had in stock. They were all ranging in height. Some being as tall as ten centimeters to as small as three. Most of the figures were of women in straw dresses with dried up flower petals in their hair. There was one oddity though. A warrior figure. Wooden armor and an iron trident that was worn and rusted by now. There was an insignia on his back, possibly belonging to the god, Poseidon.

I placed it back on its stand after analyzing its strange departure from the rest of the dolls and left the shoppe without purchasing anything from their stock yet again. I knew that most of it was forged by modern hands given the materials they were each made from. The flowers in the female dolls came from the Netherlands. Crocuses, I believe. The warrior had been carved from driftwood, making it difficult to discern the source, but not impossible. It certainly wasn't from an olive tree. The wood was still pliable, thin, and likely came from a kind of birch tree. I never doubted the beauty of the craft since each of the figures were well defined, but I did question the authenticity since the owner claimed each of them came from this very island. A blatant fib.

While my mind was in a daze, I accidentally found myself walking through the front doors of the inn and was met with an eager, crooked smile from Beatrice. She looked a tad sleep deprived from the bags under her eyes, but she was quick to comment on my own fatigue before her own.

"Edward, how are you? You certainly look better than you did last night!"

I nodded. "Nothing some new clothes and a cup of coffee couldn't fix."

I waved her toward the door, and we started walking through the city once again. Thankfully, the sun was starting to come out of hiding and the sky held no clouds ahead of us. The temperature was a bit cold, and the air was as humid as ever, to which we discussed the recent unpleasant days in terms of climatology. Finally, I found a short stone bench beside the Roman fountain I had seen earlier in our trip and we both took a rest.

"So?" She had clearly been holding all of her questions back for some time now and I was shocked that it had taken her this long to approach the subject of her studies.

I paused, giving myself time to think. "Well, I hope you'll appreciate what I have to say. Yet, I must warn you that what you learn must stay between the two of us. Understand?"

She nodded. "I just want to know what you're not telling me, Edward. It's not like we don't know one another. I was a tad hurt yesterday by your terseness with me."

"And, Beatrice, I must apologize for that. I have been a right ninny as of late."

"We all have those days, Edward."

"Not like this." I brushed her comment off. "Nevertheless, your research into the third altar has been stellar in comparison to what others have come up with. I believe your identifying the goddess behind the stand is a worthy topic for a research article. If you wished to proceed with that, then carry on."

"However?"

"However, I have uncovered some hidden truths myself. Secrets which might support your cause. Perhaps, give weight to the claims—"

"It's about Sappho, isn't it?" Beatrice cut me off before I could finish my prepared speech.

My face froze in silence and Beatrice sighed with a silent victory. "When we last spoke," she said, "you ended our talks with her. I knew that you found something! What was it? A poem? A drawing?"

I shook my head. Then, in a very cautious tone, "There are things you must be made aware of, Beatrice. Firstly, that I cannot tell you what I have learned. That would only jeopardize both your research and me honoring promises I've kept for separate parties. Secondly, if you want to continue your research, then you must not inform anyone else from our expedition what you have discovered. And lastly, I am bringing you in on an ancient secret. I expect you will help me in my own endeavors."

She was hesitant before answering, weighing my words carefully. She seemed split over the whole situation, but then she looked at me with the same curiosity I carried, and I knew that she had made up her mind. "I'd love to, but I'm not sure what you would want in terms of favors. Do you want to put your name on my paper?"

"Heavens no!" I was almost offended and let out a laugh at the thought. "No. I simply want you to listen. Don't be opposed to any new ideas, as I have already done. Instead, I want you to hear what these other parties have to say. And then, tell me if you believe them. That is all."

She seemed equal parts confused and ready for another adventure, one beyond the borders of the temple grounds site. Finally, she spoke with a brave expression. "I'll hear it out!" Beatrice smiled her British grin, and I knew that I had made the right call in bringing her in on this secret. Despite what Ekaterina and the sisters will say.

Before I could doubt my decisions and dwell on the consequences of my actions, I hurried Beatrice and myself back to the inn where we grabbed our steeds from the local stables and rode off to follow the dirt path towards Myrine's hut.

We never said a word, instead choosing to listen to the rush of the wind as our horses appeared to lift off the ground more easily. It was said that the natives would give whiskey and ouzo to the mares in order to make them run wild and compete in drunken races. I had hoped that this wasn't the case for their newfound endurance, instead believing that they might be reincarnations of Sappho and Cleis, intent on getting their story told correctly for a change.

Only half an hour later and we soon reached the small homestead of the elderly Myrine, which Beatrice found both intriguing and homely. Tending to the flowerpots, Ekaterina was quick to spot me and raise a snarl across her lips. Yet, it all melted away when she noticed that I had brought a companion along with me this time. Their eyes locked with one another, studying each other carefully like sculptors eyeing up a cut of marble. The cold air between me and Ekaterina softened ever so slightly, and I found the courage to speak up.

"Pardon me, Ekaterina. I know the rules of our agreement prohibit others of my team learning of your sisterhood, but I am imploring that I might bring Beatrice with me on this day. Another set of ears would be quite beneficial for my research. There are few people I can trust in this world, but she is one of them. I hope you will understand."

"I see," she was still a little star struck.

Beatrice lowered herself from her mare and joined us. I assisted in the introductions, but found my presence was no longer needed. Both of them started to make small talk almost instantly.

"Is Myrine home?" I asked, butting into their idle chatter.

Ekaterina nodded. "I must warn you. When you left yesterday, she was quite displeased with your behavior. I suggest that you apologize for your outburst."

I nodded. "Yes, well, I will be in need of Beatrice so that she might hear Myrine's story."

"Oh, that's quite alright. I can tell it to her while we wait out here," Ekaterina smiled. She was never one to smile while I was around. In fact, I was ready to believe that she was just another miserable person.

Beatrice seemed excited at the thought and so I left the two of them out front. As I entered the hut, I cursed myself. The plan that I had constructed this morning was to bring

Beatrice along so that she might hear Myrine's story and pair it with the notes which she had gathered from her studying the third altar. Beatrice had shortly become more knowledgeable of Sappho's history simply from asking around and I wanted her along to see if she believed Myrine's tale. Now, that plan was already in disarray, and I would be right back where I was yesterday.

Myrine was in the kitchen this morning, wearing a yellow blouse under her favorite gray shawl that I had seen her wear before. She was busied over a bowl of dough, shaping and testing its texture to see if it would make for a good loaf of bread. Her eyes lit up as she noticed me enter her hut, but then fell back to work nonchalantly.

Ekaterina was right. Myrine lacked that wry smile on her wrinkled lips. She was obviously upset over my overreaction yesterday. I announced myself yet again with the clearing of my throat.

"Myrine. I don't want to interrupt, but I have been so callous towards you as of late. I'd like to apologize for my behavior."

"You're forgiven," she stated, bluntly.

She started to roll out the dough on her countertop and measure up equal lengths. Her coldness towards me was not unwarranted and I thought of leaving back out the front door to return another day. Yet, I didn't have any days left. This was my last chance. My actual last chance.

To Myrine's shock, I took up a position beside her and started to knot the dough up. She seemed slightly perplexed, but soon accepted my help. We knotted the dough, twisting almost around each length to create small braids. It wasn't difficult to recognize Greek easter breads. Especially since there were loaves in Mytilene's bakery that I visited this morning. The process was mostly me following along with what Myrine did, whether it was molding the dough or placing seeds on top. Soon, we each had two separate loaves ready for the oven.

"Thank you," Myrine smiled finally.

I nodded. "Yesterday, I failed to keep an open mind. I… well, it's hard not to doubt everything. Constantly." I felt tears at the backs of my eyes, but persisted, nonetheless. "I came to Lesbos hoping to do things right. Find an artifact, form a theory with evidence, and write a good enough article that most people won't even read. And, instead, I-I just—"

"It's okay." Myrine embraced me, her body felt like tree branches wrapping themselves around me, protecting me from the sun.

"I believe you, Myrine. I believe every word you've told me so far and, well, I'm afraid of the story's end. The tragedy of Sappho is something every student learns about and to pull the rug out from under them… well, just look at how I've reacted!"

She looked up at me, with something more like resolve rather than confidence. "Let them think what they think. I welcomed you here because I knew that you would listen and that is all I have asked from any of my sisters here on Lesbos."

She pulled away and started to dig around in her pantry for something.

"I know that you didn't doubt what I had told you, Edward. That isn't who you are. No, you doubted yourself and how you could tell a tale that wasn't yours to tell."

She returned with a paper, old and weathered. It was scrawled with chalk, as if someone had copied a stone tablet on its surface. Myrine held it out to me.

"Well, between you and me, this is our story. You know now and that makes you family. And Sappho and Cleis would want the world to know that they escaped this island

and their people. That they ran away one night to the

Balkans, where they loved one another even after they grew

old and gray.”

I looked down at the sheet of paper and looked back up at

Myrine. She seemed to admire the warmth in my

expression as I realized what I had before me. I was blown

away. Nothing in my wild imagination could have prepared

me for something like this. It’s paper suddenly became

more delicate, and I feared for its safety.

Never had I thought that I would hold such an ancient

poem in my hands, let alone one done by the illustrious

Sappho!

“You can’t be serious!”

“I am.”

I hugged her again with all my heart. "Thank you, Myrine. I will tell your story. And they will hear Sappho's and Cleis' beguiling words once more!"

She said something in ancient Greek that I couldn't quite understand, but I took it to be a blessing from her and her sisterhood. Then, I left the hut while she placed the loaves in the oven to bake.

Chapter 15

Beatrice was beside the hut helping Ekaterina tend to the lilies with a cherished grin which illuminated even more whenever she looked up at her new acquaintance. The two were both quiet, choosing to enjoy the other's company rather than break their comfort with needless conversation. Of course, I was the one who ended that moment shared between them when I left the hut. Beatrice seemed disappointed that I had spent so little time with Myrine, apologizing to Ekaterina that she must be on her way. They shared a glance, lingering on each other's eyes for some time before Beatrice and I saddled our horses and left back for the temple grounds.

She was surprisingly quiet on our return trip, and it was me who inevitably broke that cursed silence between us.

"Did Ekaterina tell you of Sappho and the island's sisters?"

She nodded along with her mare. "Yes, Kat walked me around their little village, and I met with Carissa and Lyra. They all seemed nice and appreciated my theory that Cybele was the goddess worshipped at the third altar. We talked a lot about seafood which was strangely enlightening."

"Kat?" The name felt strange on my ears given how tense my last few meetings with her have ended.

"Oh," Beatrice almost blushed. "I just shortened her name, is all."

I nodded.

Beatrice quickly interjected before I could say anything else on the matter. "So, did you learn what you wanted to from Myrine?"

"I knew what she was going to tell me."

"Then, why did you visit her again?"

"Because I needed to hear her say it. And I needed to listen to it, truly listen, this time."

Soon we arrived at the dig site and came across a strange occurrence. Every student appeared to be there huddled up near the center of the temple. It was an odd sight and we tied up our horses as fast as we could so that we might figure out what the whole commotion was concerning in our short absence.

Oliver noticed our approach and made some room for us to see what was going on in the middle of the crowd. We arrived and Beatrice was the first to turn her head aside in disgust. I was more bewildered than anything.

Standing like a Greek hero upon one of the remaining marble pillars around the first altar for Zeus, Adrien Fischer raised his arms up into the air with a curious tool of sorts in one hand. The crowd applauded victoriously, egging on Fischer to pump his fists yet again. As he posed, I looked a touch closer toward the tool and found it not to be a tool at all, but a wooden figurine.

No. Not any wooden figure. The warrior figure from the antique shoppe!

"Colleagues! Friends! Fellow archaeologists! Today, we struck gold! Through a tiresome and difficult expedition, our efforts have been rewarded. For today, I have uncovered a telltale find! An ancient Greek wooden doll carrying the mark of Poseidon. Poseidon, the kraken king of the seas at my back! He is now, without a doubt in my mind, the prideful god worshipped at the mystifying third altar!"

Another round of cheering. Beatrice looked downtrodden, watching all of her research crushed by a false discovery. I thought of telling her it was fake. I wanted to tell all of them that the warrior figure was a phony, but I chose to bite my tongue and bide my time. Fischer and I now possessed a shaky relationship after the drunken confrontation we had last night. I needed to carefully approach this situation in order to diffuse the false hope he was now providing for these youths.

"Together, you all and I have made this possible. Our names will be known to the field for what we've found, and I promise that all—" Fischer spied me looking on in disgust, and his smile turned deceitful. "—all of you who have made an effort and worked here at my side will have their name attached to my journal article!"

Another round of cheering, especially Oliver who tried to make his voice heard over the rest of the crowd. At that point, my patience had reached its limit. I pushed through the mob and their uproarious cheering and approached Fischer's foolish grin which I wanted to knock clean from his face. Yet, I stopped myself. The students were watching us. Their applause had faded to a murmur.

This situation required caution. To reveal the truth to the crowd would only break their spirits even more. The man who had brought them down to this stripped site would be shown as a fraud and all of their efforts would be meaningless. Worst of all, I feared that their passion for the preservation of history would falter, even die out, if they came home empty handed.

Then, there was the troublesome Adrien Fischer. There was a part of me which still felt bad that his talents were wasted on his unethical standards. If we were to return to England without a discovery, then his name would be forgotten, and his career would be over. I was not prepared to ruin another man's livelihood and there were aspects of Adrien which I rather envied. The man had the skill to inspire an entire class of future archaeologists and that was something our field desperately needed. Yet, this wasn't the way to go about driving hope in the next generation. With lies and unlawful procedures which have poisoned many of us in the field already.

I was running out of time to make a decision and all those doubts which had stopped me from pursuing my passion returned tenfold. The thought of failure overwhelmed me. I felt that I would have to simply walk away and let Fischer feed his dream to the crowd. However, the feathery pages of Sappho's poem in my satchel came to mind and cleansed those anxieties which kept my true self imprisoned for so long.

Finally, I made the choice of subtlety refuting Fischer's claim. Not with my own claims, but with the words of the tenth muse of the ancient world. For only those who might listen would understand the weight of her words and realize what true discoveries entailed. Not reckless abandon, but patience.

I cleared my throat. Elevated my pitch. And embraced the

voice of a long dead poet with, I suspected, her blessing.

Cybele, our fiery mountain mother, giver of life eternal,

may I trouble you one last time.

For I wish that the raucous mirth of sinful warriors and

spiteful old kings

would lie silent with militant Pericles in Hades

so that I can lay with my darling, Cleis.

Her breath, the flickering lightning in my bones,

and I feel Aphrodite's laughter ripple, her skin the brush of

velvet.

Our hands lock Stygian, wrapped in silk, and we reach our

inferno,

as the crested larks whistle in harmony at the moon.

Before the eve of morning, I want to whisper my fatal affection

in her delicate ear once more, once more the litanies of Eros entertain,

but the land of politics and boorish men alike can be cruel to blossoming lilies.

So, I must ask you, Cybele, Magna Mater, to quiet the voices for only the briefest of moments

so that I might sing my heart's song to my only love with peace of mind.

Or else, take my voice and the trouble it has brought back to the cradle

so that I might be born and love again.

Everyone was silent, stunned, and Adrien was both lost and aghast at my own performance of Sappho's final poem. Most of the students were confused, a few recognized the fragments and were stunned to hear the whole poem read aloud. Yet, it was Beatrice who was the most awestruck. She was beyond moved by the lyrics, especially since it proved past any doubt that her claims of Cybele being the owner of the third altar were in fact true. This poem confirms that Sappho and her sisters worshipped Cybele and were compassionate for this mother goddess. It demonstrated that they likely built this altar to her, choosing to worship a god of their own rather than the affronting Zeus or Dionysus. She marveled at me, and I couldn't help but grin back.

I turned around to see that Adrien was still standing atop the marble pillar, holding onto his fake idol as it had now become his lifeline. There was no evidence he could use to defend such a fabrication and, therefore, no reason to tear him down from his stoop. His eyes weren't filled with rage as I had feared it would come down to a fist fight. Instead, I saw the panic and desperation take hold of his irises, expanding outward. I waited for him to heckle my find,

claim it a fake as his own. That also didn't happen.

Perhaps it was the shellshock of hearing the ancient words

sung or maybe he realized somehow that the poem I read

was written by the poetess herself. Either way, he remained

silent. He never raised his voice at me while I parted the

crowd with Beatrice at my side and left to pack my things

for the journey home.

Whilst we rode back into town on our mounts, Beatrice

assaulted me with a thousand inquiries into how I came into

the ownership of an original Sappho poem and why the

sisterhood would part with it. I answered her tersely.

"They wanted the world to hear the real Sappho."

That ended our talk forthrightly. We reached the inn and I

started to pack up my things. Tomorrow was our last day in

Lesbos, and I did not intend on wasting my time at the dig

site. So, I placed all of my tools and notes in my suitcases, set out some clothes for tomorrow, and decided to stay in my room for tonight. I still had some left over peinirli, albeit a little cold and messy from its time in my knapsack. Whilst I dined on my leftover supper, I took the time to drag out my copy of *Tess of the D'Urbervilles* which I had almost forgotten about during my stay on the island. There were so few pages left and I found myself easily sucked back into the world illustrated by Thomas Hardy.

It was aptly stopped by a knocking on my door. The city outside my window had grown dark in the time that I had spent reading through the novel and my visitor's knocking had abruptly disturbed me from my story.

More knocking. Rougher this time.

I knew that if I prayed it wasn't Adrien Fischer, then I would be disappointed. So, I didn't. Still, I was quite perturbed when I swung the door open to see his scowling face in my doorframe. There were few words I had for the man.

"Evening, Adrien. I hope all is well."

He was fuming and he still held onto that false idol in his hands. "Edward, you bastard! Why can't you let anyone else achieve anything? It's always about you, isn't it? Today, I found—"

"Please," I scoffed, "I've allowed your charade to carry on, easing the worry in those poor student's you've fooled, but don't you ever try and pull something like that on me! Anyone with half the training you have would be able to tell that you purchased that figurine and buried it on the temple grounds. I'd like to believe it wasn't true! That you did achieve this discovery as a collective, but shame on you! You have become just like Gessler! Shame! Only shame can come from your efforts, not the delusion you've created for yourself and those aspiring to be like you!"

At this point, Fischer reeled his hand back, the one holding the warrior figurine, and hurtled it at my chest. Its wooden exterior made for an uncomfortable impact, which had me stagger backwards, but I held my ground and unwaveringly stared at Fischer.

His face, once expressing his hate towards my revealing his lies, was beginning to lower itself in his arms. The man began to weep with tears flowing rapidly from his eye ducts.

"Please, Edward! You must understand. You of all people must understand! I can't lose my reputation at the journal. This will be the end of my career! Please!"

I looked down at the now misshapen warrior figurine. Its trident was broken in three splinters across my room's floor and his head had shattered upon impact with my torso. I wondered if the antique shoppe could repair him in his condition.

"Edward, you've found that poem! Right? Why don't you be a pal and we bring it to the journal together! You can take the credit. I don't even care about having my name attached at this point! Please, just help me out of this mess I've created!"

At this point, I looked up at the groveling, pathetic figure in my doorway. Fischer was nothing like the man I had met on the docks of Brighton. That same desperation which I once faced, he now shared in. And in a moment of petty pride, I shut the damn door in his face and cleaned up the warrior from my floor. He wailed a little while longer outside of my door, but even that soon ceased.

Chapter 16

I went to bed early last night to catch up on some much-needed rest, but also because I planned on waking up early in the morning to say farewell to Jayson and the olive workers before my boat ride home. Sadly, my eyes didn't open until the sunlight was streaming through my window. Quickly, I dressed myself in a beige work shirt, stone grey pants, and my nice Oxfords. In a flash, I was out the inn door and rushing off to the café. Yet, when I arrived, I was disappointed to find that none of the workers were drinking their coffee. I cursed myself for not keeping a better track of time and started to head back to the inn when I caught sight of the wagon rolling past. Jayson and his men were sitting on the back with their tools in their laps and cracking wise as they liked to do.

"Jayson!" I waved my hands frantically.

He heard my cries and pointed me out to the rest of his gang of workers. Each of them waved their goodbyes back at me and I couldn't help but continue until they were well out of the city limits.

I smiled. My worries were washed away, and I was relieved to find that I had the chance to see my friends one last time before I left Lesbos. With that checked off my list of things to do, I decided not to waste any time on the other items on my directory. I hurried over to the stables and untethered my usual mare from the pack. She was a bit giddy today and I provided her with an apple from the local market which I had picked up on my way over.

"One last ride, girl?" I asked her.

She was delighted and I feared that she might rush off without me. I saddled her and together we rode up the dirt path one final time. My thoughts were mostly preoccupied on the journey. I found myself trying to photograph the landscape in my mind so that I might keep the beauty of my time here in my memory long after I returned to England. The wonderful forests. The eclectic architecture. The cliffs…

As I was passing the crags by the temple grounds, I stopped my mare.

Standing hunched over in the center of the dig site was none other than Adrien Fischer. The man had a demon inside of him with the way his eyes were constantly skirting the edges of the tree line while he dug away at the turf beneath his feet. His clothes were filthy, and he carried himself mostly on his shovel, favoring his left leg. Likely he had tripped over something in the night and now walked with a limp.

While I was stopped on the dirt path, he looked over to me whilst ripping up the floor of the second altar to Dionysus. We stared at one another. For him, this was another showdown, and I noticed the veins on his neck bulge as he was prepared to shout at me once more.

I pitied him. Despite being well aware of the kind of leech Adrien Fischer could be, there was only pity in my heart for him on this morning.

And so, I simply rode up the dirt path and never looked back at him again.

I soon reached the village on top of the largest hill on the island and many of the women were scurrying around this morning doing chores and planning their days out with one another. They paid me no mind as I strolled into their village center and slowly approached Myrine's hut. I was almost at the door when I caught sight of Beatrice and Ekaterina beside a beech tree nearby. They were nestled closely in the crook of a tree branch, studying the finer details of the others' face, and occasionally they giggled like school children. However, their faces relaxed into one another, finding the softness of their lips, and sharing a stirring kiss that made my cheeks burn red from simply watching. I averted my gaze with my own smile and knocked on the door to Myrine's home.

There was a short call from inside and I took it as a sign that I might enter. The hut was warm with a small fire in the fireplace to offset the cold air of dawn. Myrine was relaxing in her wooden chair, weaving some kind of colorful green and purple blanket across her lap. She plastered that wry grin as soon as she recognized me in her living room.

"Edward, it's nice to see you back."

I took a seat across from her. "Sadly, I must inform you that this is my last day on the island. I wish that I could stay a little longer but…"

She nodded. "It's quite alright, Edward." She gestured toward a plate of koulourakia cookies which I reckoned she made yesterday with the leftover dough. I gladly helped myself to one of the braided biscuits. "I feel like, when we get older, it's not how much time you spend with others, than it's how special that time is spent."

"Each moment is special," I argued, "It's just a matter of when or if it is a concern to us."

"That's a rather selfish way to look at things," she laughed.

"Yeah… well, I guess it is."

We shared a few silent minutes listening to the crackling of the fire. Myrine continued to knit, and I enjoyed another one of her cookies. Something about this home just felt different from the rest of the island. No. It felt different from the entire world. Perhaps because I had never been welcomed with such hospitality from a stranger before. It was inexplicable, but I didn't want to leave. In a matter of days, I had somehow felt a connection with this woman more so than my own flesh and blood. Each time we met; I instinctively knew that I was cared for.

I didn't realize that we were both smiling at one another again until Myrine's voice shuttered away my own thoughts.

"Keep the poem, Edward."

Although I wasn't thinking about the work at the time, even now Myrine could tell what anxieties my subconscious was struggling with. I was taken aback by her blunt reassurance.

"I'm going to bring it back to this island. After I've shown it to the world, I promise to return here one day and give it to the sisterhood. You have my word."

She didn't pay my response any mind. Myrine stood up from her seat and set aside her half-finished blanket and knitting needle. I stood up to meet her and we both embraced in a farewell hug. We didn't speak. Our thoughts were enough. And I left the hut without any regrets.

Outside, I was met by both Beatrice and Ekaterina who were taking a short stroll through the village. Beatrice spotted me and rushed over on her own to greet me. Her hair was still in tangles and her smile was spotted with crooked teeth, but there was an effervescence about her that made Beatrice glow.

"Hello, Edward!"

"Beatrice. Came to say your goodbyes?" I nodded over at Ekaterina who was idly waiting by the beech tree.

Beatrice was quiet. Her face shifted along with the weight on her feet. She slowly found her own voice.

"N-n-no. Actually… I think, well, I think I might stay here a while longer."

When the words were done with, she looked aside to avoid my gaze. To her surprise, I rested my hand on her shoulder and grinned.

"I think that is a lovely idea, Beatrice."

Her shock only added to her glow. "Really? What about the paper? My research on the third altar? Aren't you going to talk me out of it?"

I shrugged. "Don't worry about your paper. You can write it and send it over to the journal whenever. I don't think that they will have an issue with you wanting to spend some more time here. Besides," I nodded over at Ekaterina, "there are far more important things in life that can't be kept waiting."

Quickly, Beatrice reached around me for a hug, and I patted her on the back to help with her excitement. "Thank you, Edward," she said. "For understanding."

"Of course," I nodded and sent her on her way back to Ekaterina.

The two love birds waltzed through the patch of lilies around Myrine's home before skuttling off back into the forest. I waved them off before saddling up on my mare once again to head to the docks of Mytilene.

As our boat left shore, I couldn't help but feel a little melancholy about the whole expedition. The trip was so much quieter without Beatrice there to share in poking fun at Fischer's ego nor someone whom I could confide in concerning my worries about the field. Although the students seemed to have drifted away from Fischer's tall tales, their hesitancy toward their future studies was palpable. I may not have destroyed their hopes of an early success in their careers, but that didn't mean they weren't disheartened by following the orders of a fool. I feared that they would soon be plagued by the same doubts I had possessed going into this adventure and that they wouldn't have the support of people like Myrine or Archie to guide them forward.

Which is what made Beatrice's departure sting the most to me. I knew that she had to stay. But she was the brightest hope for the future of this field and now she was gone.

How could anyone hope to put in as much effort as she had

in her studies?

I found no answer. My sleep was restless the whole trip

back to England and any attempt to put pen to paper on

what I had discovered was impossible.

Chapter 17

After a few days of travel across the continent, I soon arrived in Brighton's docks where construction on the new world had continued in my absence. Similar styled buildings had sprouted up beside the striking urban brownstones which I had criticized prior to my journey. The presence of more unsightly outcroppings created for a bittersweet welcome home.

As I was nearly out of Brighton, a carriage pulled up alongside my own and the ghostly face of Adrien Fischer leered at me through the carriage door. We had avoided one another on the long train rides through Europe's countryside and I was shocked to see how unwell his features had become in a matter of four days' time. His lips moved, but there was no voice which accompanied it. His whispered curses fell on deaf ears over the rustling of our cages and the whinnying of their respective horses. Then, he knocked on the roof of his ride and the driver sped off on a parallel road heading east. I waited until I was sure that Fischer was gone before relaxing into my seat.

Along my carriage ride back to Somerset, I attempted to write in my journal what I had discovered in my time at Lesbos. Yet, I still had nothing to write about. Or, rather, I lacked the courage to write upon my travels. Perhaps it was Fischer's curse on the carriage ride or maybe my binding doubts had returned after I had left the island. Either way, I couldn't come up with a single word no matter how much valor I mustered in my pencil.

I had hoped that this idleness which had cursed me prior to my expedition would have subsided upon my return home. This didn't seem the case. I spent a day at my writing desk. An entire day. The only thing I had written was:

In a recent expedition to Lesbos, a team of archaeologists have uncovered…

I had scrapped even that right before I turned in for the night. There was less time than ever for me to finish my research article for the *Archaeologia* and I still couldn't manage to write what I had found.

The next day, I never even set foot in my study. Instead, I had reclined over in my living room on my much-missed high-back chair with Hardy's *Tess of the D'Urberville's*. I finished the work within an hour and searched my library for something else to entertain my procrastinating mind until the right words would come to me. I settled on a work that I had discovered some weeks prior to my departure in a local Somerset bookshop from an American author, Kate Chopin. The librarian had looked at me funny when I had picked out *The Awakening*, clamoring about its vulgarity and that it was something disagreeable.

To which I replied, "Then it must be a good book." And I paid for it from my coin purse and left for home. Now, I opened the first page and was lost in its story for hours.

The day ended with me nowhere closer to finishing my article and I had just about accepted my fate when a familiar knocking occurred on my door the very next day. Admittedly, the last day I had to write my article.

I opened it to see the white fluffy hair of my close friend, Archie, with his maroon umbrella in hand. I had been so preoccupied with my writing, or void of writing, that I had failed to see that it was starting to rain, pouring down at a violent rate from the storm clouds above. I, also, realized that my estate was quite cold and that I had forgotten to light a fire this morning.

Archie could tell from my disheveled appearance everything that was now racing through my mind, and we skipped over the casual greetings.

"You forgot about our teatime yet again, haven't you?" Archie smirked.

I nodded. "Yes. I am afraid that it must have slipped my mind."

I waited for his upsetting sigh, a heave of hot air, before he stepped past me into the foyer. Archie set aside his coat and umbrella on the hooks nearby.

"I'm quite shocked you haven't died from neglect, Edward. I mean, good heavens, how have you made it this long—"

I quickly enveloped him in a hug. Partially to shut him up, but mostly because I missed my friend terribly on such a lonesome journey and desired his support once again. He hugged me back in kind and his tone became much gentler.

"How about you put the kettle on, and I'll start up the fireplace. We'll have a nice chat in the living room."

"That would be wonderful."

I set off to the kitchen and busied myself with preparing some black currant tea for myself and Archie. There wasn't much in the way of biscuits or finger foods, so I decided that the tea would have to do on its own. When I heard the whistle of the kettle, I poured the piping hot water into each teacup slowly, measuring out a little more for myself as I usually did when Archie came over. The black currant tea was surprisingly strong with an aroma of fresh berries wafting through the halls of the kitchen. I placed the two cups of tea on saucers and carried them out to the living room where Archie was sitting in a short fiddle-backed velvet chair. He accepted his cup with a nod and sipped it silently.

"Mmh. Your collection of teas never ceases to delight me, Edward."

"I picked it up on my last adventure through the Indus valley the previous year. I've been meaning to try it."

I took a sip of the hot, fruity drink and was surprised by its aggressive flavor. Perhaps a vanilla leaf tea would've been better for our noontime.

No matter. I placed my teacup aside and noticed Archie was watching me. Right, I had promised him that I would recount my story and findings to him when I returned home. Still, where do I begin? What do I tell him? Do I leave the sisterhood out? Christ, I was at a loss for words. I felt like this expedition was impossible to write down, let alone recount to anyone who wasn't there.

"Edward," Archie noticed my frustration. "I know that look. It's the same, I fear, as when I last saw you here in your home. Am I correct in assuming such?"

I nodded once, but then shook my head. "No. No, I don't think it is."

"Well, what is it then? Do you care to tell me the events of your journey or not?"

I shut my eyes and breathed a deep sigh. My mind had organized the story close to a million times in a million different ways since I left the docks of Brighton weeks ago.

I was constantly trying to catalogue and record what was happening, mostly because I was afraid that I would get the whole thing wrong or fail in finding anything of importance. That worry needed to end. Now.

I stood up from my chair and began to pace to and fro across my rug in the living room. Archie watched me like I was a mad man.

"I left for the docks of Brighton with the intention of finding something on the island of Lesbos. And, although the site was barren, I did make a peculiar discovery…"

And then, everything started to come free from the chains of my memory. I told Archie of Adrien Fischer and his destruction of the Sanctuary of the Three Gods. I recounted how I came into the discovery of a secret sisterhood who found strength in the readings of Sappho. Then, I informed Archie of the story which Myrine described to me on the first day I visited her at her home. And then, I unsheathed the scroll of papyrus from my knapsack and shared it with Archie. His eyes nearly jumped free from his skull at the sight.

"This is an incredible find, Edward."

"The sisters were quite generous, Archie. They simply want the world to hear the truth about Sappho, so as to dispel the rumors that have plagued them for centuries."

"And will you send it to a museum?"

I shook my head. "No. We have no right to this work. Once finished with my writing, I plan on sending it back to Mytilene where it belongs."

"Well, it sounds to me like that will make an excellent article, correct?"

I paused. I stopped in my tracks and stared out the window, studying the rain falter its violent torrent on the land. It had nearly petered out in the time it had taken me to recount my tale.

Archie repeated himself in case I had not heard him. But I had. Still, I possessed no reply.

"Edward?"

"Archie, I don't think I am going to write that article."

"What? Why on earth would you not? You've gone through the trouble and, you said it yourself, the sisterhood wants you to share it with the world. Why wouldn't you?"

I turned to face him.

"When I left Lesbos, I left a good friend behind. Beatrice stayed behind, gave up the field. I have yet to meet any student with the same potential as her. What does that say about the field, Archie? It's turned into a right mess, it has."

Archie was now the one to raise his voice towards me. "Now you listen here, Edward Davenport! You know damn well that I felt the same way when I was turning up loose stones and sharing my knowledge with students like you. I nearly gave up on my career when I was stormed out for my own research. But then, I met you. You, who have shown me some of the most amazing finds I have ever laid eyes on. Look at this poem," he thrusted the papyrus in my hands. "The world would never have found it if I hadn't sent you down to Mytilene! And who's to say there won't be another Beatrice or, heaven's forbid, another Edward Davenport!"

He smiled, resting a reassuring hand on my shoulder.

"Perhaps the archaeologists who are practicing right now might not see your wisdom, but they will. One day. You can't give up hope on them, Edward."

I looked down at the poem in my hands and felt the warm presence of Myrine at my side along with Archie. Although she wasn't here, I knew that she would agree with him.

"Perhaps you're right."

Archie huffed. "Of course, I'm right. Now, let's figure out this article of yours."

"No," I said.

He stopped from sitting down in his chair again, clearly ready for another argument, but I shook my head.

"I do agree that this discovery and research must be shared with the community," I clarified. "But I will not submit to the *Archaeologia*."

His face drew inward, slightly confused, and I gestured for him to take a seat. He did so and I took my own across from him. My tea was still warm, and I refreshed my palette with another sip of the black currant liquid.

"I'm afraid that you have me at a loss, Edward."

"I'm meaning that we don't send the article to the journal whose standards are lacking and support the same treasure hunters and glory seekers who have destroyed thousands of ancestral sites. I won't conform to their unethical practices.

Instead, I suggest that we create our own scientific journal. One where we are more selective of what is published, and we assist our colleagues who understand the lawful practices of archaeology. Archie, you are most certainly right. There are ways to change the system. But we need to stop permitting others to dishonest our study."

Archie was stunned. His teacup was resting in the palms of his hands, ready for him to take another sip. Yet, my offer of a joint venture, seemed to have filled his appetite. Then, that old smile returned to his face, and he set the teacup aside.

"Edward, I think that might be the most brilliant thing you've ever done."

"No, Archie. The most brilliant thing that I've done so far."

We shared a laugh and spent the afternoon discussing plans as to how we would go about establishing our own journal. Archie had contacts in the publishing business which he would reach out to tomorrow. I thought of Beatrice and figured that I would write to see if she would send her article to me instead of the *Archaeologia*. It was a start and we both seemed satisfied with our work until the next day. I walked Archie to his carriage and returned to the study. Suddenly, I found the urge to write.

In a recent expedition to the island of Lesbos, I was met not with the dust and fragments of an aged temple constructed by warring men, but with the kind words of a brilliant woman. Sappho.

To Be Continued in *The Lost Maps of Valverde*